A WHISPER IN THE SHADOWS

BOOK TWO
OF THE
CHILDREN OF ADHIREN DUOLOGY

AMY SMART

A WHISPER IN THE SHADOWS
Copyright © 2024 by Amy Smart
All rights reserved.

Contact: amysmartbooks@gmail.com

ISBN 978-1-7383221-3-8 ; 978-1-7383221-4-5 (Ebook)
978-1-7383221-5-2 (Hardcover)

First Edition: May 2024

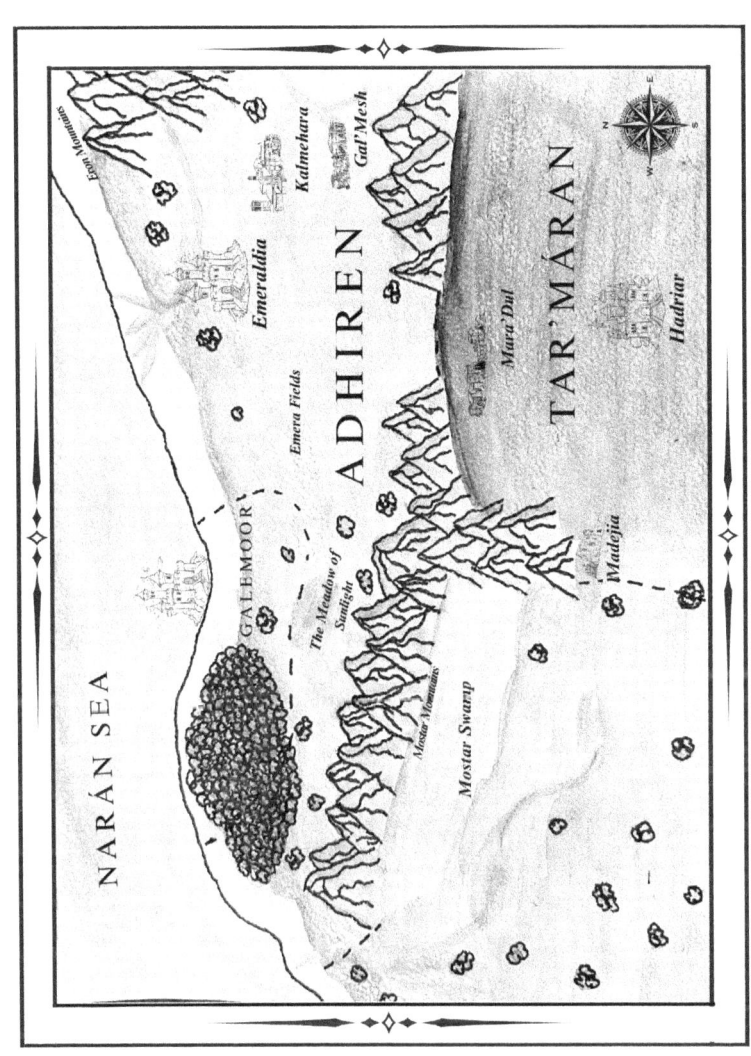

NARÁN SEA

Exon Mountains

Kalmehara

Gal'Mesh

Emeraldia

ADHIREN

TAR'MÁRAN

Mara'Dul

Hadriar

GALEMOOR

Emera Fields

The Meadow of Sunlight

Madejia

Mostar Mountains

Mostar Swamp

CHAPTER ONE

"COME ON!" VANESSA GRASPED Naara's hand tightly as the two of them ran through the burning forest. "We have to run faster!" Their feet pounded on the hard dirt trail as the sound of drums echoed in the distance.

"I'm scared!" the little girl cried.

Vanessa stopped for a moment to wipe a tear from Naara's face. Her little pink dress was stained with dirt and ash from the fires.

"We're going to be okay," she said, gasping for breath. "The Doves are watching. But we can't stay here. If we stay here, Malik will get us, and we will die. We have to keep running. Do you understand?"

Naara nodded solemnly.

"Alright then, let's go."

"Wait!" Naara halted. Vanessa nearly fell over.

"What's wrong?" Vanessa asked, letting go of Naara's hand. The little girl stood as if she had turned to stone.

"I have to wait for my parents," she said.

"Call out to them!" Vanessa said frantically. "Tell them to run! They will catch up with us! You can't go back now."

"I have to go back," Naara's voice sounded distant. Her movements were stiff and unnatural-looking as she turned to head back to her burning village. Her faraway stare was void of the light and mischief Vanessa had grown to love.

"Naara, no." Vanessa pulled on her friend's arm but she wouldn't move. "They are coming. They will catch up to us. We have to run!"

"I cannot come with you." Her stare was unnerving.

Vanessa turned away for a moment, trying not to cry. There was a loud snap, and a giant, flaming tree branch fell between the two girls.

"Naara!" Vanessa called, choking as she breathed in the smoke. She frantically waved her hands around the fallen branch. "Naara, are you okay?"

Silence. No sign or sound of the little girl. Then a faint "Vanessa!"

"Naara!" Vanessa called again. The world began to sway beneath her and fold into darkness.

Vanessa sat up with a start. Someone was calling her name, but it wasn't Naara.

Her father was standing in the doorway of her bedroom. She was home. She wasn't in the forest.

"Are you okay?" Alexander asked.

Vanessa sighed and placed her head in her hands. It had been two years since the tragedies that occurred in her quest to save her people from Malik's tyranny, but the memories were as fresh as if they had just occurred. Almost every night she woke up like this, and every time her father was there.

"Another nightmare?" he asked.

Vanessa nodded solemnly. "Naara."

"I'm so sorry, honey." Her father sat down on the bed and put his arm around her. "Whatever happened, and wherever she is now, we have to trust that Aric and his father are taking care of her."

"If she survived," Vanessa asked, wiping away a tear, "wouldn't Aric have brought her to Adhiren by now? Wouldn't we have seen her?"

"That would make the most sense," Alexander admitted. "But I don't know for sure. As you told me from your conversation with the High King, we won't always know the end of everyone's journey. At least not until we are in the Kingdom of the Sky ourselves."

"I wish he would at least let Naara send me a message," Vanessa sniffled, "to let me know if she is okay."

Silence hung between Vanessa and her father for a few moments before she spoke again.

"Why does it hurt so much? It feels like I can hardly breathe."

Alexander wrapped his daughter in a warm embrace. "The pain of losing those you love never truly goes away, Vanessa. Some say it gets better with time, but I don't know if that's entirely true."

"Do you still miss my mother?" Vanessa sniffled.

"Of course. I wish I could have saved her. I know there was nothing I could do, but that regret will still follow me for the rest of my life."

Vanessa pulled away from her father's embrace and met his serious gaze. "Do you think what happened to her was unfair?"

"Yes, I do."

"Sometimes I think I will never feel normal again." Vanessa sighed and stared down at the ground.

"You have been through a lot, Vanessa. You will never be the same girl you were before you came looking for me. Our past leaves marks on us, much like your scar."

Vanessa reached up to feel the raised mark on the back of her neck, where a dark soldier had injured her in the Battle of the Emera Fields.

"They are there to show what we have been through," Alexander explained, "and what we have overcome, by the grace of Aric. It took a long time, but your scar healed. Now most days you don't even notice it. Though we don't always realize it at the time, these difficult things we go through make us stronger."

"Do you think the others have nightmares about what they went through and everyone in our village that we lost?"

"I wouldn't be surprised if they do. But as you've started to see, everyone deals with these things differently. As much as you can, you need to be there for each other. Even when it feels hopeless, you are never alone."

A light tapping noise at the window interrupted their conversation. Vanessa and her father looked up to see a familiar white bird with glittering wings peering in. They opened the window and let it inside.

"Is everything alright here?" the Dove asked. "I sensed you were in distress."

"Yes, we are okay," Vanessa replied as she wiped her

eyes with the sleeve of her nightgown. "It was another nightmare. Thank you for checking on us."

"Any time," the Dove replied. "We are always here to help!" The majestic bird chirped and flew away into the night.

Through every rise and every fall, the Doves will hear and see it all.

Vanessa pulled the sheets back up to her shoulders and took a deep breath.

"The Doves are watching us," she said.

"Always," Alexander replied. He gave Vanessa a kiss on her forehead and went back to bed.

* * *

The next morning Vanessa and her father, along with most of Kalmehara, trudged out onto the Emera Fields for another day of battle training. While Adhiren was at relative ease with its neighbours, King Aric stressed the importance of always being prepared for battle.

"You will never know everything there is to know," he would say. "Every day soldiers both young and old will find they are learning something new. That is how we stay ahead of our enemy—we never stop learning. When we assume we know enough, that is when Malik is most likely to strike."

"Good morning, Vanessa," Brianna's cheery voice rang out in the frosty air.

"Hi Brianna." Vanessa gave her friend a hug.

Brianna pulled away from the embrace and looked her friend in the eye. "What's wrong?"

"Nothing." Vanessa looked at the ground and kicked the dirt with her foot.

"Another nightmare?"

"Naara." Vanessa nodded and refused to make eye contact with her friend, lest she start crying. "I miss her so much. The nightmares are getting worse, Brianna. I'm afraid I might be going crazy."

Brianna put her hand on Vanessa's shoulder. "I'm so sorry. Please let me know if I can do anything to help. I'm always here for you, you know that." She gave Vanessa her biggest and brightest smile. "And you are definitely *not* crazy. At least, no crazier than the rest of us."

Vanessa laughed and gave her friend another hug. "Thanks, Brianna."

"Hey Vanessa!" a little voice called out. It was a young redheaded boy, running across the field toward her at lightning speed. He had a huge smile on his face and was waving around a small wooden sword. He was one of the soldiers' kids, no older than five. He stopped to catch his breath as he met her gaze. "Can you teach me some sword fighting skills today?"

"Not today, Eamon," Vanessa replied, forcing a genuine-looking smile. "I think Tarak has some very specific plans for training today. Maybe you could join Caleb and I some evening this week and we could practice then?"

"Okay," the boy replied. He took off back toward the city to join his friends. "I can't wait!"

Vanessa sighed. She liked Eamon and his enthusiasm to learn was very encouraging, but she constantly worried that she would mess up and accidentally teach him the wrong thing. He and the other children would carry that with them all their lives and would have her to blame. *I'm only thirteen! They have so much trust in me. I don't understand why.*

The clip-clop of the hooves of Tarak's horse approaching snapped her out of her self-pity. The training session was about to begin.

"Listen up," Tarak's voice rang across the field. All chatter ceased as Aric's Army turned to listen to one of its top commanders. "I know you have all been working very hard lately and your strength is beginning to fade, but we must not stop training now. Malik and his army may attack at any time, and I do not want it to be said of us that we were not prepared. Today we will focus on one-on-one combat. You will practice your attack and defense skills using the swords that Aric has given you, which should be by your side at all times. Pair yourselves up, experienced soldiers with apprentices. Long live the king."

"Long live the king!" the crowd cheered in reply with as much enthusiasm as they could muster.

As Vanessa looked around for someone to train with, she spotted Jareth standing off to the side of the group. His arms were folded across his chest and he was staring at the ground.

"Hey," she greeted her old friend with a smile.

"Hey."

"I haven't seen you around much lately. What have you been up to?"

"Nothing."

"I haven't seen you at training."

"I haven't been coming."

She was shocked by that response. *Why would a loyal soldier of Aric not want to show up for training sessions? I know we're all tired but we've all committed to serve our king. I've never heard of anyone deliberately skipping training before.*

"Well I guess you've got a lot to catch up on," she replied in her best cheerful voice as she nudged him in the arm.

"Yeah, I guess." Clearly Jareth was not feeling up to conversation on the subject.

"So, wanna train together today?"

"Sure, whatever." He looked up at Vanessa and gave a halfhearted smile.

I'll take what I can get. Vanessa shrugged. She and Jareth found an empty space where they drew their swords and began to practice.

Vanessa soon noticed that Jareth wasn't only lacking a positive attitude. His swordsmanship had dwindled severely since they last trained together. He failed to block nearly every mock attack that came his way, even the really simple ones. When another soldier made a comment about it and Jareth looked like he wanted to kill him, Vanessa suggested that they move further away from him and the rest of the group nearby.

Jareth seemed fine with that decision, but still hardly spoke to Vanessa for the entire day. *Maybe it's a guy thing. Maybe he doesn't want to talk about his feelings and things like that. I'm sure if something is really wrong he would tell me or Gaerwin.*

"Do you want to come over to my father's place sometime for dinner?" Vanessa asked. "He's a really good cook."

"Maybe." Jareth sighed. He kicked the dirt with his right foot.

"Okay, well, let me know whenever you want to come over. You're welcome anytime."

"Okay."

Something's off. Vanessa thought. *But what is it?* Wanting to escape the awkward situation, she said goodbye to Jareth and went to find her father.

* * *

"So how did training go for you today?" Alexander asked his daughter as he sat down at the table and handed her a bowl of vegetable soup.

"I saw Jareth," Vanessa said as she put a spoonful of soup in her mouth.

"Oh really? How is he doing? I heard he was doing an apprenticeship in Emeraldia with Aurelio, the jeweler."

"I don't really know," Vanessa replied between bites. "He didn't want to talk much. He hasn't been hanging out with Dillan or Gaerwin either."

"Hmmmm. It could be that he's dealing with things differently than you three," Alexander commented. "Like we discussed the other night. Keep trying to reach out to him if you can. I'm sure he needs his friends right now more than he lets on."

"He needs to practice his sword fighting skills more than he lets on too." Vanessa laughed. "It was almost comical watching him in training today. Until he got that angry look in his eyes..." She decided to switch topics. "How was the training day for you?"

"It was pretty good," Alexander replied. "I met a young apprentice named Korbin. He said his younger brother Eamon is, to quote his own words, 'one of your biggest fans'."

"Ah yes." Vanessa chuckled. "I told him he could practice some sword fighting skills with Caleb and I later this week. He's a great kid and all but I'm still not used to having 'fans'."

"Well," Alexander said as he finished off his meal. "We had better clean up and get straight to bed. Another full day awaits us tomorrow."

"Father," Vanessa asked as she helped to clean up the supper dishes. "Have you ever heard of a soldier in the Army of Aric choosing to skip training sessions because they didn't want to go?"

"No, I can't say I have," Alexander replied. "Some days I feel like resting instead of training, but those feelings have never stopped me from showing up to defend the country I love. I can imagine it is the same for the other soldiers. Why do you ask?"

"I was just curious," Vanessa said.

"You need to get to bed," Alexander said as he placed a hand on Vanessa's shoulder.

"I'm really not looking forward to that."

"You know I will always be here when you need me." Alexander kissed his daughter on the top of her head. "Maybe tonight the nightmares will stay away."

"I hope so."

Vanessa and her father bid each other goodnight. She turned and headed to her room, shuddering as she braced herself for the terrors that would soon invade her dreams.

CHAPTER TWO

VANESSA AWOKE TO BRIGHT, warm, rays of sun. As she blinked her eyes and stretched, the darkness from the night before began to fade away. There was no battle training today. She, Dillan, and Gaerwin were going to enjoy their day off relaxing in the Meadow of Sunlight! She quickly grabbed her things and headed for Emeraldia, where her friends would be waiting for her. Together they rode their horses to the first place in Adhiren they had ever visited.

Vanessa chose to focus on the beauty of the meadow, trying to forget the tension she felt from her frequent nightmares. She picked a small purple wildflower and wove it into the intricately designed crown of asters, hydrangeas and marigolds that she had been working on for the past hour. The little purple flower was a small jewel in the midst of the bright blues and yellows. She took a breath and smelled the sweet scent of fresh green grass she had woven into her creation. She adjusted a couple of petals here and there, and decided she was satisfied with the result. She placed the crown on her head and turned to face her friends. "What do you think?" she asked.

"I think about a lot of things," Gaerwin replied, staring at the sky. "Like what I'm going to have for dinner tonight. Or what I'm going to have for breakfast tomorrow. Or when the next banquet is going to be. People say guys don't have much going on in their heads but really…"

"Ahem." Dillan nudged Gaerwin and nodded in Vanessa's direction.

"Oh, the crown!" Gaerwin added. "It looks okay I guess."

"I think it looks lovely," Dillan replied.

He thinks I look lovely! A gentle breeze whipped Vanessa's long, brown hair in front of her face, blocking her vision. She desperately tried to blow the hair out of her face, while her friends laughed at how ridiculous she looked. She barely suppressed a giggle herself as she finally pushed the hair out of her eyes. She readjusted herself and then sat, blinking, and posed as if she were a rich lady at a fancy party.

"I think it looks better with the hair out of your face," Gaerwin added.

"I've made these crowns for years," Vanessa said, "but none of them are ever the same. There are so many different types of flowers in the meadow, and it makes for endless combinations. This really is the most beautiful place in Adhiren, don't you think?"

"It sure is," Gaerwin said, snatching the crown off Vanessa's head and placing it on his own. He made a silly face and mimicked Vanessa's pose of a rich lady. "The Meadow of Sunlight truly is a remarkable place. It's also the best place to spend a day off from training."

"Hey, give that back." Vanessa reclaimed her creation and held onto it with both hands. Gaerwin smirked. Dillan laughed and then shoved Gaerwin over as revenge for bothering Vanessa.

"The meadow was the first place in Adhiren that we saw," Dillan added, "I remember back then I didn't think it was even real. It was so big, so beautiful, and so full of light."

"And one of the first things you wanted to do was have a race," Vanessa recalled.

"Yeah, and I *won*."

"I believe it was a tie."

"She's right," Gaerwin interjected.

"Whatever."

"Remember our first banquet at the palace?" Gaerwin asked, his blue eyes wide with wonder. "It was the best feast in the world. I ate so much I felt sick for a week after. The fact that I had barely eaten for days before that probably didn't help."

"I'm glad you've gotten your eating habits back under control since then." Vanessa paused and stared at the horses that were grazing nearby. She was silent for a moment before she asked, "How often do you think about them?"

"The horses?" Gaerwin asked with a puzzled expression.

"No," Vanessa replied, "the people in our village we had to leave behind. The ones who died in the fires."

"Not very much." Gaerwin shrugged. "You, Jareth and Dillan were my closest friends growing up, and the others were so rude to you when you came back. I mean sure, I miss my parents..." he paused for a moment and his expression went blank. Vanessa placed her hand on his shoulder.

"...But there's nothing I can do to bring them back." He shook his head and shoulders as if trying to rid himself of a pesky bug, but Vanessa knew it was more likely a painful memory. Gaerwin didn't like to have serious conversations. It made him uncomfortable.

"I'm doing my best to move on and focus on what I have now. Like my friends, the palace, and all of those amazing banquets."

"I miss my parents too," Dillan replied softly, looking at Gaerwin. "Sometimes I have dreams about them. And I think about the other kids we grew up with. How their lives would have been so different if they were able to come with us."

Vanessa sighed and closed her eyes as a single tear rolled down her cheek. Dillan looked up at her.

"You did the best you could," he reassured her. "We all did. We will never forget them." He placed his hand on Vanessa's shoulder.

The three friends gazed at the clouds without saying a word.

Gaerwin broke the silence by jumping up and pointing to Dillan. "Guess what you *did* forget today."

"I don't know. What?" Dillan replied nonchalantly.

"It was your turn to clean the stable by the marketplace." He punched his friend playfully in the arm. "I just remembered you told me that this morning."

Dillan jumped up, filled with urgency. "I need to go back. Right now. Or my mentor is going to kill me."

"Let's make a game of it," Gaerwin suggested with a smirk. "Last one back to the city gates has to clean up horse poop?"

"You're on," Vanessa said as she mounted her horse.

"You seriously think you're going to beat me?" Dillan said to Gaerwin as he rolled his eyes.

"Hey you never know. Miracles happen."

"On your mark, get set..."

"Hiyah!" Vanessa put her heels down and urged Shadow forward.

"No fair," Gaerwin groaned. "Come on Esperanto, let's go. We *have* to beat Dillan!" He made a clicking noise and tightened his grip on his horse's reins.

The three friends rode through the Meadow of Sunlight as fast as their horses would take them. Vanessa was in the lead, followed closely by Gaerwin, until they got closer to the edge of the Emera Fields. Then Dillan began to inch forward, vying for first place.

"Better hurry up Vanessa!" he called.

"Come on Shadow, go faster." Vanessa urged her horse as the gates of Emeraldia came into view. Shadow's hooves kicked up grass and dirt as she approached the finish line. Vanessa hollered and cheered, letting go of Shadow's reins. Lamenting whines and groans came from Dillan and Gaerwin, who were not too far behind.

Vanessa turned to face her friends, who were moving slowly compared to how she flew with Shadow.

"Ha! How the tables have turned. Now I can outrun both of you." She reached down and patted her horse's head affectionately.

"Need. More. Practice!" Gaerwin gasped as his horse slowed to a trot. Dillan arrived at the gates only seconds before him. "You've been riding like this longer than us."

"Excuses, excuses..." Vanessa waved her hand toward them, dismissing the comment with a smile. "Have fun cleaning up the stable."

The three friends paused to take in the beauty of Aric's city, which shone like gold in the afternoon sunlight.

"Emeraldia sure is beautiful," Dillan sighed.

"It really is," Vanessa replied. "But sometimes I wish it had more trees."

Dillan and Gaerwin agreed. The village where they had grown up, which had been destroyed two years before, had been in the middle of a forest. As beautiful as Adhiren was, sometimes the country did not fully feel like home to them. They were still getting used to so much open sky.

The three friends dismounted their horses and led them into the city.

"Have you seen Jareth around lately?" Vanessa asked Dillan and Gaerwin as they walked.

"No," Dillan replied. "I think he moved to a different place in the city recently. Every time I've asked him to join us he's said 'no' or made up another excuse. Maybe he doesn't want to hang out with us anymore."

"We should find out where he lives and visit him

sometime," Gaerwin added. "Maybe he's forgotten how awesome we are."

Dillan laughed. "Yeah, we should do that. I'll ask around."

By now they had reached the market square. It was the social hub of Emeraldia, especially on sunny afternoons. The smell of fresh baked bread combined with various spices wafted through the air and made Vanessa's mouth water. All around them people were walking back and forth, calling out the items they were selling: "Candles! Wax candles half price today"; "Apples! Come and get your fresh apples!"; "Authentic rugs woven in Gal'Mesh! You won't find them anywhere else. Today only!"

Swarms of children ran about between the vendors, chasing each other and laughing. Occasionally one would charm a vendor into giving them a free sweet treat or fresh piece of fruit. Vanessa remembered wandering through the market in Kalmehara for the first time when a curly-haired blonde blue-eyed boy named Alexander ran past her, dashing her hopes that her father was at the marketplace. That was when she didn't know where he lived, and before she met King Aric. So many things had changed since then.

It didn't take long for an enthusiastic mob of small children to find her.

"Vanessa," they called. "Tell us a story!" She snapped her focus back to the present moment.

"Settle down," Vanessa replied. "You're going to scare the horse. I need to put her back in the stable and then I will tell you a story."

With beaming faces the children followed Vanessa to the stable and chattered among themselves as she tied Shadow up and gave her some food to eat. Dillan and Gaerwin tied up their horses as well, and Dillan headed home as Gaerwin got to work cleaning the stable. He gave Vanessa a pitiful gaze as she turned to leave.

"You'll survive," she said with a smile.

Once she returned to the market square, Vanessa took a seat on the ledge of a fountain while the children gathered around her. "What story will it be today?"

"The one about the High King!"

"Haven't you heard that one before?"

"Some of us have. But some of us haven't."

"It's a *really* good story."

"Okay," Vanessa acquiesced with a smile. "The High King story it is."

Cheers erupted from the group as Vanessa began.

"It all started when we were fighting a battle against Malik and his dark army, on the Emera Fields. At first, I was doing pretty well at fighting them off."

She made swooshing noises and pretended to wave a sword back and forth.

"You've seen Malik?" one child asked.

"Is he really scary?" another inquired.

"Yes, he is," Vanessa replied. "But Aric isn't afraid of him so I try not to be."

"Woah."

"Then a dark soldier came behind me and bam! He struck me, and I fell over."

A few gasps of shock came from the children.

"Everything went dark, and I didn't know where I was. But then the darkness went away, and the sky was bright like it is right now."

A couple children tried to look up directly into the sun and ended up covering their eyes.

"I noticed that I wasn't hurt, and that I wasn't wearing armour anymore. I was wearing a beautiful white dress."

"Oooooh!"

"It was kind of like I was floating, but moving forward at the same time. Eventually I came to a city gate and there was a man standing there. He looked like King Aric but older, and much wiser. He wore a crown and had the kindest blue eyes."

"The High King of the world?"

"Yes, that's right," Vanessa chuckled. "He shook my hand and welcomed me to his kingdom. It was so beautiful. Sparkling buildings more beautiful than the Emerald Palace rose in every direction and the lake I saw was shimmering as clear as glass. It was all very nice, but then he said something I did not expect."

"What did he say?"

"He said that I was still needed back in Adhiren, and so I had to come back. But he also said that one day I could go back there and see him and his kingdom again. So he sent me back. When I first opened my eyes, it didn't make sense. I could see blue, and some blurred shapes, but it took a while for me to realize I had come back and my father, my friends, and King Aric were waiting for me."

"Did you die?" one child asked, wide-eyed.

"No. Yes. Well, sort of."

"That is so cool."

"I want to see the High King," another child said. "He sounds nice."

"And his kingdom sounds so beautiful," a little girl added with a dreamy look.

Vanessa laughed. "You will one day. If you choose to serve Aric and join his army, it will be a place of rest for you as it is for all the soldiers who have gone before us."

"I'm going to join Aric's Army when I'm old enough."

"Me too."

"But isn't it dangerous?"

"Yes. It can be dangerous. Aric's enemy, King Malik, and his soldiers are determined to hurt us and bring destruction to our land. But that's why we fight him, to keep our land peaceful and strong."

"I want to be like you when I grow up."

Vanessa smiled at the child, but inside she cringed. *If only they knew the pain I have experienced and the sacrifices I've had to make to be here, they would not be saying such things.*

When the childrens' parents began to call for them to head home, Vanessa stood up and turned to leave.

"Will you tell us another story?" a little girl begged, grabbing onto Vanessa's dress.

"Another day," Vanessa replied with a smile. "Right now I need to head home."

Vanessa waved goodbye to the children and went to get Shadow from the stable.

Alexander was finishing cleaning up from his supper when his daughter walked in the door. She had been living with him in Kalmehara since she came to find him two years before. He smiled as she told him about her day, an occurrence which had been much more common. He had been so much happier and energetic since she and her friends had returned to Aric's country. It was as if his life now had meaning, and he made every effort to make the most of every day. He even started cleaning his house on a regular basis, which was a shock to his neighbours. A roaring fire in the kitchen was warming the entire house, and he had saved her some soup and bread.

When they finished catching up on the day's events Vanessa and her father went to bed early. Army training had been quite rigorous as of late and they needed all the rest they could get. As Vanessa wrapped her blankets close around her head, she took a deep breath and smiled. It was so wonderful to have a city like Kalmehara to call home, and to finally know where she belonged. While she would never forget what it felt like to be out of place, confused and afraid, those memories were beginning to fade into the background of her life. Now there was so much light, life and joy. She wished the sunshine and warmth of the day would last forever so she wouldn't have to endure the terrors of the night.

CHAPTER THREE

VANESSA WAS IN THE DARK. As she took a step forward a tree branch slapped her in the face.

"Ow!" she exclaimed, putting her hand to her cheek. She was bleeding. She shuddered in disgust and kept moving forward. Pushing back another branch, she saw her friends and family from her village standing in a clearing with their weapons drawn. Eshana was holding her two children tightly, whispering to them and trying to keep them from crying.

Drums were pounding in the distance. She knew exactly where she was and what was about to happen. The glow from her necklace was nearly blinding.

Malik, disguised as a man from the Redtree Village, jumped out of the bushes and ran straight for her. She would never forget those horrible eyes. She had seen them so many other places before. With a battle cry he pinned Vanessa to the ground and ran a spear through her arm. It burned like fire, and sent the burning sensation rippling through the rest of her body.

She screamed in pain, but Malik would not relent. With a smirk, he drove a second spear into her other arm.

She tried her best not to cry. She closed her eyes for a moment and repeated to herself: "it's just a dream, it's just a dream..." but it felt so real. Those evil eyes piercing her soul. The deep-throated unsettling laughter. The cries of her friends and family around her.

Malik grasped the collar of her dress and pulled her closer toward him.

"You will never win," he hissed. His hot, pungent breath overpowered her senses.

"You think this is bad? It's only the beginning. You're no match for me. None of you puny humans are." He released his grip and Vanessa's head landed on the ground with a thud.

With a start, Vanessa sat up and opened her eyes. Malik was gone. The battle had ended. Her arms were aching and she was covered in sweat. *It was just a dream, it was just a dream...* but was it? Of all the terrors she'd endured in the nights since her return to Adhiren, this one felt the most real. She had looked into the eyes of Malik. It was the same in this dream as when she'd been a prisoner in Hadriar. But that didn't make any sense. Malik wasn't there. He was in Tar'Máran, plotting the destruction of Adhiren. *He can't be in two places at once, can he?*

She looked around her bedroom, trying to regain a sense of calm. She was safe. There was no more danger. Everything was in its place, except in one corner. A dark human shape that appeared to billow like a cloud of smoke hovered by the door. *My eyes must be playing tricks on me.* She gave her head a shake and then whispered, "Dad, is that you?"

A low hiss came from the mysterious shadow. Vanessa gasped and pulled her sheets close to her chest.

"This isn't over," an unfamiliar voice spoke, sending chills down Vanessa's spine. And then, as suddenly as it had appeared, the shadow vanished. Vanessa desperately wanted to go to her father for comfort, but he had slept through this nightmare and she knew he needed the sleep. She looked out the window and saw a Dove perched there. It met her gaze, nodded, and then flew off quickly as if it had an urgent message to deliver.

* * *

The Emera Fields were buzzing with excited chatter the next morning as Vanessa and her father joined the rest of the Army of Aric.

"Have you heard?" Brianna exclaimed, running over to her friend. "There's going to be a soldier naming ceremony tomorrow."

Vanessa couldn't help but share Brianna's excitement. She never tired of attending the ceremonies. It was always exciting when new soldiers joined the army, and there was always a great feast and celebration that followed. Every event at the Emerald Palace was better than the one that came before it.

"How many people are being named?" Vanessa asked.

"Seven. Four adults and three kids. From what I've heard, they came to Emeraldia on a diplomatic errand from Galemoor. They were amazed that the people here are actually kind and that Aric hosted them generously at the palace. They've decided to renounce the lies they were formerly told and join Aric themselves."

"That's great."

"I know, I'm so excited!"

It would be a new experience getting to know more people from Galemoor. While technically a city within Aric's realm, it had its own king and queen and a government that functioned separately from the rest of Adhiren. The king and queen disliked Aric so much that they forbade their people from hearing stories about him or meeting him in person. For this reason, Vanessa and her friends did not know much about the city or the people that lived within it. She remembered the little redheaded servant girl and her mother whom she waved to on her way back to Emeraldia two years before. That, and meeting her friends Tarmon and Corwin, had been her only contact with anyone from there.

In light of this announcement, many people found it difficult to get back to work and meet their training objectives for the day. Who wanted to focus on training when there was a banquet to prepare for?

Vanessa and Brianna walked away from the crowd and sat down to pick small wildflowers that grew near the edge of the field. Much to Vanessa's surprise, no one complained or made any remarks about how she and Brianna were supposed to be helping the younger apprentices.

While they were in the midst of a conversation about what to wear to the ceremony, Alexander appeared and greeted them with a smile.

"Good morning, Mr. Handeraz!" Brianna said.

"Good morning, Brianna," Alexander replied.

"We're only taking a short break," Vanessa said, looking up from picking wildflowers. "We will get back to training soon, I promise."

Alexander laughed. "That's perfectly fine. I'm not here to get you in any sort of trouble. I was wondering if I could borrow Vanessa for a moment?"

"Of course." Vanessa stood up and followed her father.

"King Aric has just spoken to me about an exciting opportunity," Alexander began, "and I would like your help."

"What does he want us to do?" Vanessa asked, curious.

"As you may have heard, there are three young people who are going to be named as soldiers in the Army of Aric tomorrow night. They are going to need mentors."

Vanessa gulped.

"Aric has asked me to consider mentoring one of them, and to have you join me in this task."

Vanessa stopped and stared at her father with her mouth gaping open.

"I know, I know," Alexander chuckled. "You are still a new soldier yourself. And you still have much to learn!

I will still be your mentor as well. We would work together, as a team."

"I don't know…"

"You have been through a lot in these past few years," Alexander said, gently placing a hand on Vanessa's shoulder. "But I have also noticed that you have been developing great wisdom and leadership skills as a result of your difficult experiences. Aric told me that he thinks you are one of the most skilled young soldiers in the army."

Vanessa was stunned. *How can I be one of the most skilled? I'm certainly not the strongest. Why does Aric think I can do this?*

"First and foremost, you are my daughter," Alexander reassured her. "I will not force you to do this. But Aric thinks you are ready to help in such a role. And if you decide you are ready, I would love your help."

"Of course," Vanessa nodded timidly and stared at the ground. She didn't want to let her father down.

"We'll talk about it more when we get home tonight," Alexander said. "Why don't you go back with Brianna and get in a bit of training before lunch?"

"Okay," Vanessa looked up and smiled at her father. "See you later!"

When Alexander had disappeared from her sight, Vanessa went to tell Brianna the news.

* * *

"This one?" Vanessa asked, holding up a bright yellow

dress to show her friend. Golden embroidered flowers spread and bloomed from the base of the flowing skirt to the shoulder on one side. It was very elegant, like something a princess would wear.

"No, I liked the blue one better on you," Brianna replied.

Vanessa held the blue dress up again. It was a more simple design, light and dark blue fabric with a silver waistband and long, flowing sleeves. Yet it held a degree of elegance in its own way.

"You're right," Vanessa agreed.

"That's what I'm here for." Brianna's blue eyes lit up as she smiled. As long as Vanessa had known her, Brianna always had a closet full of beautiful dresses. Vanessa now had some of her own, as her father had been committed to providing her with the best wardrobe he could afford once she made her decision to stay and live in Kalmehara with him.

Brianna sat on Vanessa's bed in a long pink dress, readjusting the colourful flowers she had placed in her blonde, wavy hair. She always looked beautiful no matter what she was wearing.

"I can hardly believe," Vanessa said, "that two years ago I didn't even know what a soldier naming ceremony was. And I didn't have anything to wear."

Brianna laughed. "We've come a long way since then haven't we?"

"Yeah." Vanessa stared at herself in the mirror, holding up her dress. She remembered the first time she met Brianna in the Meadow of Sunlight. Brianna was wearing a clean, beautiful dress and her own had been as worn out and filthy as an old rag.

"Sometimes it doesn't seem real."

"It does sometimes seem too good to be real," Brianna admitted, "but I'm so glad it is. I can't imagine living under a cruel ruler like Malik." She shuddered. "It's almost time to leave. I'll go get my family and we'll wait for you at the front door." She jumped off Vanessa's bed and headed to the kitchen. Vanessa quickly got dressed and ran out to join the crowd headed to the Emerald Palace.

* * *

As Vanessa followed the crowd into the Great Hall for the soldier naming ceremony, she found her friend Nimeesha. Together they were able to find a place to sit that was right near the front of the throne room. They were close enough to the tables in the centre of the platform that they could see the jewels on the ornamented crowns.

"Remember when we were up there?" Nimeesha asked. Her dark green eyes shone with excitement and the memory of the night of her own naming ceremony.

"Yeah," Vanessa replied with a laugh. "They look just as nervous as we did."

"I probably haven't said this enough," Nimeesha turned to face Vanessa, "but thank you for being there for me that night, and in the months that followed when we had to fight against my parents. I have met a lot of wonderful people in this army but not all of them are as good of a friend as you are."

Vanessa gave her friend a hug. "You're most certainly welcome. Although I have you to thank as well. It was your determination to speak to Aric and learn more about his army that got me to this ceremony in the first place. I wouldn't have been here today if it weren't for you."

A trumpet call commanded the silence of the audience. All eyes turned to King Aric as he stood at the centre of the stage, dressed in white clothes and a crimson cloak. Everyone stood up to show their respect. Aric's face was beaming, as it always was during a soldier naming ceremony.

"Greetings, members of my army and other esteemed guests," he began. He motioned for the audience to be seated. "It is an honour to welcome you to this ceremony. Today we welcome guests from the city-kingdom of Galemoor. They arrived in our city on trade business only a week ago. After meeting some of you and seeing the unity of our soldiers they requested a meeting with me to learn more about us and the purpose of my army. The rest of the trade caravan was not interested in this and they have headed back to their home. But these seven people have decided to renounce the lies told them by their former ruler and become members of my army, and this country, today. They will henceforth be under mine and my Father's protection. I trust you will welcome them with open arms."

"We will do as you say," Khalon, one of Aric's top commanders, said as he kneeled from his front-row position near the table of crowns and swords. The crowd cheered enthusiastically.

Aric turned to the Galemoorians. "You have shown great courage in your decisions, and it is my privilege to welcome you here today."

Vanessa watched the movements of the people on the stage who were about to be named. They were all dressed in such fine clothes that she could not tell who had previously been in the Galemoorian upper class and who had been a servant. Six of them stood in a line facing the audience, turning occasionally to smile at each other, all on equal ground. One younger Galemoorian stood slightly behind the others. Vanessa couldn't see her well, as she could only make out the bright red colour of her dress.

There was a tall, slender woman with pale skin and soft blue eyes. Her long golden hair was adorned with a pink flower crown that matched her dress. She was chattering excitedly to the man beside her as she held his hand and gestured to the crowd with her other hand. *He must be her husband,* Vanessa concluded. The man had light brown skin and short, wavy hair similar to her father's. He was dressed in a fine suit of navy and gold. He nodded and smiled. Beside him stood a man with dark skin, short black hair and kind brown eyes. He stood stoically, taking in his surroundings with the occasional nod to the crowd and a gentle smile. He was wearing a suit of white and gold. Beside him stood a woman with wild red hair and freckles. She wore a dress of dark green and brown and a colourful wildflower crown. She mostly kept to herself and offered the occasional timid smile. *The people of Galemoor are so beautiful!*

Next Vanessa turned her attention to the three young people, who were standing the farthest away from her on the stage. There were two boys and a girl. The boys were standing next to the rest of their group, while the young girl in the red dress stood behind them. The first boy had dark skin, black hair and bright green eyes. He had the biggest smile as he whispered to his friend beside him and pointed at the sparkling crowns and swords on the table. The other boy, pale with brown hair and brown eyes, nodded excitedly as his friend continued to talk. The first boy turned and reached out a hand to the timid girl, offering a friendly smile, but she refused his invitation to step forward. The young girl had brown skin, long, black wavy hair and the most intense green eyes Vanessa had ever seen. She was small in stature, and kept glancing around the room as if she was not fully aware of why she was there. Occasionally she would tremble as if she were cold. She looked down at her feet rather than meeting the gaze of the audience. She gripped the fabric of her red and gold dress in one hand and drummed her fingers against her leg with the other. *She's probably overwhelmed,* Vanessa thought. *It is a lot to take in all at once.*

"We won't waste another minute," Aric concluded. "Let the naming begin! Lady Katharine, please step forward." The woman with the long blonde hair stepped forward to declare her loyalty to Aric and his cause. She beamed from ear to ear the entire time, occasionally glancing back at her husband who would be named after her. She was given a dainty silver, sparkling crown with green and blue gems. One by one the other adults came forward and were Named: Lord Raheem, Omari Mbabazi, and Maribeth Taylor. Then the two younger boys, whose names were Juwan and Seth, came forward and received their crowns. As the trembling young girl stepped up to the centre of the platform she knelt and lowered her face to the ground. This was a rather odd behaviour that Vanessa had never seen at a naming ceremony before. *Why is she so afraid?* With a warm smile, Aric knelt down and placed his hand on her shoulder and encouraged her to stand.

"We are all equal here," he spoke in a soothing voice. Then he whispered something to the girl that Vanessa couldn't hear.

As the young girl rose to her feet, she met Vanessa's gaze for a moment. Her expression was like that of a timid animal. Vanessa felt sorry for her, but knew in a couple of minutes she would be alright and would probably feel much happier. She gave her a reassuring smile as the girl turned back to face Aric.

"Will you, Arimay Radjani, Daughter of Lailani, of Galemoor, now choose to be, both now and forever, a member of the Army of Aric and of the High King? Do you promise to remain faithful to the army and its cause?" Aric smiled warmly at the girl and she offered a timid smile in return.

"Yes," came the quiet but confident reply. Arimay kneeled and Aric tapped his white glowing sword on both of her shoulders. Her eyes widened and Vanessa recalled the moment at her own ceremony where she had felt a new rush of energy flow through her veins, unlike anything she had ever experienced before.

"Then, by the power given to me by the High King, I hereby pronounce you a servant of the High King and a full member of the Army of Aric!" Arimay rose as Aric placed his crest, in the form of a colourful stamp of a Dove carrying an olive branch, on her right hand. She received a silver crown with red jewels and went to join the rest of the Galemoorians. The crowd burst into wild applause. Vanessa and Nimeesha joined in the cheering and clapping. The girl was no longer shaking as she stood between Juwan and Seth. The three young Galemoorians had their arms around each other as they looked out into the crowd.

Seven soldiers stepped onto the stage from the audience and handed each new member of the army one of the ornamented swords. Each sword and sheathe had been crafted with the specific recipient in mind. After they had received their gifts, Aric asked those who had gathered if there was anyone willing to help train the new recruits in their army-related duties, as was the custom. Experienced soldiers stepped forward and committed to mentoring six of the new recruits. Soon the young girl was the only one left. She met Vanessa's gaze again briefly as she looked around the crowded room.

Aric spoke: "Is there anyone here who is willing to step forward and train Arimay Radjani as a new soldier of the Army of Aric?"

A very long moment of silence followed. The girl looked down at the floor as if she were about to cry.

"I will," Alexander's voice rang out as he moved toward the centre of the room. He knelt and bowed before the king. He turned and met Vanessa's gaze. Before she even realized what she was doing, Vanessa was at the front of the room beside her father, kneeling before King Aric.

Aric smiled at them. "Alexander, your faithfulness to my army and its cause are a shining example to our young people. And Vanessa, you have proven your worth as a loyal member of this army in a very short time. I trust that both of you will pass on what you have learned to Arimay."

"Yes," Alexander and Vanessa replied. "We will do as you say." They led Arimay down from the stage and into the crowd. After introducing himself, Alexander suggested that Vanessa take the new soldier to meet some of her friends.

Nimeesha watched Vanessa wide-eyed, with her mouth hanging open in surprise. Her expression quickly turned to an excited smile when she saw Vanessa and Arimay heading her way.

"Congratulations!" Nimeesha said as she embraced her friend. "I didn't know you were thinking about becoming a mentor."

"Aric suggested that my father and I work together." Vanessa shrugged, not wanting to verbalise her concerns about what she had just done. "Arimay, this is my friend Nimeesha. We met King Aric together and became soldiers on the same day."

"Nice to meet you." Nimeesha held out her hand to Arimay. The young soldier started to bow her head, then saw Nimeesha's hand and reached out to shake it.

"Hi," came Arimay's timid reply.

Vanessa introduced Arimay to some of her other friends, but the new apprentice rarely spoke and often refused to meet their eyes. It was so different from how Vanessa felt at her own naming ceremony. *Hopefully that won't last forever,* she thought. *I want to make this as enjoyable as possible for her, but she doesn't look like she's having fun. Is she scared of me? I'm scared...how can I assume responsibility for someone only three years younger than me? How will I be able to stay focused while battling my nightmares?*

Vanessa caught Arimay staring at her while she was lost in her thoughts.

"Let's go find a place to sit." She cleared her throat and made sure she was smiling. Arimay stayed close to her side as they wandered around the Great Hall to speak with the other soldiers before the meal.

The dark-skinned Galemoorian man came forward to introduce himself.

"Hello, Vanessa," he said, reaching to shake her hand. "I am Omari."

"Hello, Omari," Vanessa replied as she shook his hand. "It's nice to meet you. I have not met many of your people. I'm glad you've decided to join Aric's Army."

"We haven't met many of you either," Arimay said quietly.

"It is unfortunate that our king despises the people

of Adhiren so much," Omari said with a sigh. "I hope that will change in the future."

"So do I."

"I want to thank you for mentoring Arimay." The man cast a warm glance in the girl's direction.

"It's an honour." Vanessa smiled. Arimay gave her a skeptical look.

"Arimay," Omari turned to the young new soldier. "We have set up tents for the Galemoorians in the small courtyard close to the Great Hall. You are welcome to join us there after the banquet. There is a separate tent for you, next to Seth and Juwan's tent."

"Thank you, Omari," Arimay replied with a polite nod, which Omari returned.

Omari placed his hands gently on Arimay's shoulders. "You are destined for great things, Arimay. Never forget that. I am so proud of you." The man's eyes teared up as he beamed with pride. "I will see you later. There is so much to see and so much delicious food to enjoy!" He turned and waved to Arimay as he went to explore the rest of the celebration.

"See you later!" Arimay called after him.

"He's really nice," Vanessa commented. "Is he your brother? Or your father?"

"No," Arimay frowned.

There was a moment of awkward silence before Arimay spoke again.

"None of my family were able to come with me." There was a bitter tone in her voice. "Omari has been kind to me. He looks out for me. He made sure I always had enough food to eat, and that the boys didn't bother me too much. He kind of acted like a father I guess."

"Well I'm glad you had someone looking out for you." Vanessa decided not to ask Arimay any more questions.

"Hey! There you are!" Brianna's voice rang out through the crowd. She ran over to Vanessa and gave her a hug. "Hi, I'm Brianna." She held out her hand to Arimay.

"Hi," the girl replied sheepishly. "I'm Arimay."

"Pleased to meet you, Arimay. You know, you two are really missing out on all the delicious food over there. Come on!" She grabbed Vanessa by the arm and Arimay followed.

In the midst of the festivities, Dillan and Gaerwin came running over to Vanessa, gasping for breath as if they had been running for miles.

"It's Jareth," Dillan gasped. "He's gone!"

"Gone?" Vanessa asked.

"Yeah," Gaerwin said. "We thought it was strange that he didn't come to the banquet. Even if he doesn't like training that much right now, we all know how he feels about food. We found Aurelio and asked where he was. He said Jareth didn't show up for work today and hasn't been back to his house at all, even for meals. We looked in his room and all his things are gone."

"Where else could he be?"

"I don't know. He doesn't have relatives here and no other friends that we know of. This isn't like him, even with the mood he's been in lately."

"No, it's not."

"What should we do?"

"Tell the Doves," Vanessa suggested. "They can see far more places than we can. We will have to trust them to keep an eye on him, wherever he may be."

"Good idea," Gaerwin said. He took off around the corner in search of the nearest small feathered servant of Aric.

"By the way, congrats on becoming a mentor," Dillan said, changing the subject.

"Thanks. It's pretty intimidating at the moment, but Aric seems to think I'm ready."

"You're probably way more qualified than us lowly soldiers," Dillan said mockingly with a bow. Vanessa punched him in the arm.

"Food's over there if you want any before I eat it all," Nimeesha interjected, breaking up the mock fight.

Vanessa, Arimay, Brianna, Nimeesha and Dillan raced to the nearest table filled with delicious goodies. They talked and visited with the other soldiers throughout the evening, trying to distract themselves from worrying about their missing friend. *It's up to the Doves now,* Vanessa thought. *There's nothing more we can do.*

As the night wore on, Vanessa went looking for her father. She eventually found him chatting with some soldiers who worked with him in the stable.

"It's nearly time to set up our tent," he said when he saw her. "Shall we join the rest of the Kalmeharans over there?"

Vanessa shook her head no. She stared at the

ground, not wanting to speak her fear aloud. That she would have another nightmare and disturb the other soldiers. That they would find out something was wrong with her. That Arimay would find out. *No, that can't happen.*

"Sorry honey." Alexander put an arm on her shoulder. "I forgot. We can set up our tent a little ways away from the group if you'd like."

Vanessa gave him a hesitant smile and bent down to help him carry their tent. It was decorated in the traditional bright blue, purple and red fabric of Kalmehara and had just enough room for both of them.

After they had laid out their bedding, Alexander turned to his daughter.

"I will always be here for you," he said, "Whenever you need me."

"I know," Vanessa said with a weak smile. They bid each other goodnight. Vanessa drifted off into an uneasy slumber as she worried about her missing friend and her new responsibilities of being a mentor. She didn't know that even more worrisome events were taking place in the shadows as she slept.

CHAPTER FOUR

VANESSA SHOOK OFF the chill in the morning air, which hung around her as heavily as her sense of dread from her dark dreams. It was Arimay's first day of training, and she and her father were meeting her at the gates of Emeraldia. Vanessa wasn't sure what to say to her, but hoped she could help her feel a little less nervous than she had been the night before.

As Arimay approached the city gates she greeted Vanessa with a hopeful smile.

"What are we going to do today?" Arimay asked.

"We will be doing a lot of different things in the next few days," Alexander began with a smile. "But don't worry. No one knows everything on their first day so if you feel a little overwhelmed…" he stopped talking. Arimay was staring at him.

He's talking too fast, Vanessa thought.

"Today I'm going to introduce you to one of the war horses in the king's stable," Alexander said. "You will be riding him for some of your training."

"I'm going to do *what*?"

"Ride a horse," Vanessa repeated. "You have ridden one before, haven't you?"

Arimay focused her gaze on the ground and kicked at a small rock. "No. I haven't."

"Well there's a first time for everything," Vanessa did her best to sound cheerful.

"I…" Arimay stuttered. "I don't like horses. They scare me."

Vanessa put her hand on Arimay's shoulder. "Don't worry. I'll be right there with you. I've been doing this for a few years now. If you have any questions just ask me, okay?"

The girl nodded timidly and allowed Vanessa and her father to lead her to the palace stable.

They stopped in front of a large black horse with a white patch on his forehead that resembled a star.

"This is Danilo," Alexander explained. "He looks tough, but I've been told he's a sweetheart." He reached to pat the horse's nose and he whinnied with delight.

When Arimay reached up to pet the horse, he turned and glared at her with his dark brown eyes, snorted, kicked up one of his hooves, and then turned back to face Alexander.

"He doesn't like me," Arimay stated grimly.

"Give him a chance." Alexander laughed. "You two just met. Maybe he's feeling nervous too. Aric has supervised his training and declared him fit to serve in his army. I'm sure he will behave."

The horse gave a sideways glance toward Arimay, suggesting Alexander's last comment held no guarantees as far as he was concerned.

Vanessa showed Arimay how to put on Danilo's

saddle, mount him properly, and control the reins. Then she hopped down and handed the reins to Arimay.

"Why don't you get on him and I'll get Shadow," she said. "My father will get his horse, and then we'll go out to the Emera Fields together to practice riding."

"Okay." Arimay sighed as she closed her eyes and took a deep breath. She grabbed onto Danilo's saddle, pulled herself up and swung her right leg over the horse's back. The horse shifted its weight below her, causing her to let out a muffled shriek.

"Is everything okay?" Vanessa called as she rounded the corner on Shadow. She saw Arimay's panicked expression as she held onto the reins for dear life.

"Don't worry," Vanessa reassured her, "he's fine. You won't fall off. Trust me." She leaned over on her horse to untie the ropes and open the gate that had been keeping Danilo in the stable.

Arimay's whole body was shaking. "It's okay," she said to herself. "I'm not afraid, I'm not afraid." Danilo seemed to calm down for a moment, then he reared his head and let out a whinny, his hooves scraping the dirt.

"What's wrong with you, stupid horse?" Arimay growled. She kicked her heels against his sides, unaware what message she was sending to the horse by doing so.

As if in reply, Danilo reared, trying to get Arimay out of the saddle. Screaming, Arimay grasped the reins even tighter and closed her eyes as the horse took off, galloping out of the palace grounds and heading for the Emera Fields.

With a frustrated sigh, Vanessa urged Shadow to follow the exasperated horse.

* * *

Arimay opened her eyes to see Emeraldia flying past her, faster than a flash of lightning. She could feel the steady rhythm of Danilo's hooves beneath her, and she heard the occasional exclamations of surprised Emeraldians as she shot past them in the streets. Her hair kept flying back and forth around her face, blocking her vision with patches of black. Her body bounced up and down rather ungracefully in the saddle. She could hear her heart beating rapidly as she and the angered horse neared the city gates. *This is it,* she thought. *I'm going to die.*

When Arimay was only moments from certain death Vanessa and her father pulled up beside her on their horses. Vanessa reached for Danilo's reins and the horse came to a sudden halt just outside the gates of Emeraldia.

Arimay's heart raced as her hands let go of the reins and she fell forward against the horse's neck. She closed her eyes for a moment, trying to get rid of the dizziness she had from going so fast and then suddenly stopping. Another snort from Danilo caused her to open her eyes. Vanessa had a concerned expression on her face.

"Are you okay?"

"The dumb horse tried to kill me."

Alexander reached for Arimay's arm and led her off the horse. He held onto her shoulders until Arimay had regained her balance.

"I think that's enough riding for today. Go back into the city and rest. We'll try again tomorrow."

CHAPTER FIVE

"ARIMAY," ALEXANDER CALLED from across the field, "loosen up on Danilo's reins! You're holding them much too tight. No, not that way..." He rode closer to examine his apprentice's posture.

"What if he gets mad at me?" Arimay asked, holding the reins with shaking hands.

"For goodness' sake," Vanessa snapped, "you've been riding this horse for almost two months now and he hasn't run away. He's not going to kill you. Why do you have to be so afraid of everything?"

The moment the question left her mouth, Vanessa knew she had made a mistake. Alexander gave her a look. Arimay had dropped the reins and was staring at her. Her eyes glazed over and she was about to cry.

"I'm sorry." Vanessa sighed. "I shouldn't have said that. Bring him over here. You should stay closer to me. Then if he's causing any trouble I'll be able to help you."

Arimay held Danilo's reins and led him closer to Vanessa and Shadow.

"That's perfect," Vanessa said as Arimay rode beside

her. "Much better."

I can do this, Vanessa sighed as she reined in her irritation. *I can do this. One day at a time.*

Alexander spoke up. "How about we finish with riding for today and try something else?"

A look of relief washed over Arimay's face. "That would be great."

They led their horses back to the palace stable. Vanessa reminded Arimay how to properly tie and secure the horses in their stalls. She gave Danilo a fresh apple as she walked past. The horse snorted in delight and devoured it in a single chomp. Alexander grabbed the items she needed for the next training activity and left the stable with Vanessa and Arimay in tow.

"Let's practice some basic dueling," Alexander suggested as they walked through the market square. Arimay's eyes widened.

Be patient, Vanessa told herself, *be patient. This is all new to her.* "Don't worry, I wasn't very good when I started. It takes time. We will use the wooden practice swords today."

Arimay flinched and held her hand out gingerly to grab the hilt of the wooden sword Alexander gave her. It was nowhere near as heavy as a real one, but Arimay's arm dropped with the weight of it all the same.

Since no one was selling in the market that afternoon it made for a perfect wide open space to move around in. Alexander began by reminding Arimay of some basic stances.

"It's important to keep your balance," he instructed, "or the slightest nudge from the enemy could send you to the ground if you're not prepared." He held his sword with both hands and stood with his feet shoulder-width apart, with one foot facing forward and the other 45 degrees away. His knees were slightly bent and his back was straight. "See if you can knock me over."

Timidly, Arimay walked up to Alexander and gently pushed against his right shoulder. Alexander moved a bit to fix his balance, but did not fall over.

"See?" Alexander said. "You could push me much harder than that and I still wouldn't fall over. That's because I'm balanced and focused."

"Like this?" Arimay asked Vanessa, modeling the stance she had been shown.

"Excellent!" Vanessa walked up to her apprentice and gently nudged her shoulder. Arimay was shaking but did not lose her balance.

"Okay, now let's practice blocking." Vanessa showed her apprentice how to lift the blade of her sword against hers to block an attack. Arimay was still moving very slowly and gently. Vanessa felt as if she were practicing in slow motion.

"The dark soldiers will be much stronger than this," Vanessa advised. "Put your strength into it." Arimay's eyes widened and she lowered her sword.

Okay, I'm scaring her, Vanessa thought. *I'm definitely scaring her. But she needs to learn this! How can I make sword fighting any less intimidating? Did she know this was what she was signing up for when she became a soldier?*

"Let's practice two more moves and then we'll call it a day," Alexander said. He showed Arimay how to parry and how to step away from an attack and aim for an opponent's arm.

"Come on, Arimay!" Vanessa called, still going through the motions at a pace significantly slower than her usual training, "Pretend I'm a dark soldier of Malik and I'm going to hurt you. Fight me like you mean it!"

Arimay dropped her sword and began to tremble. "I...I don't want to hurt you."

Vanessa set her sword down and put her hand on Arimay's shoulder. "You won't hurt me," she said. "I promise. I have been doing this for two years already, with *real* swords."

"I don't think I'll be very good at this." Arimay sat down on the ground and sighed.

"No one is good at anything on their first day," Alexander reassured Arimay, sitting down beside her. "Or even their first week, or first month. Even the best sword fighters in the army had to practice for years."

"That sounds like a lot of hard work," Arimay rolled her eyes. "And I'm tired."

"Who says practice can't be fun?" Vanessa said, putting on her most cheerful expression. *I'm tired too, kid. And running low on patience. But maybe this idea will work.* "I'll tell you what, let's have a contest. If you beat me in a duel with our wooden swords I have to ride Danilo tomorrow. If I beat you, you have to bring Danilo a nice treat tomorrow and tell him how wonderful you think he is. I promise I'll go easy on you."

Arimay's eyes lit up. She stood up and shook Vanessa's hand. "Deal," she said. "You're on!"

The two soldiers of Aric unsheathed their weapons.

"Ha!" Arimay shouted, stepping forward. The duel had begun.

After repeating the same moves back and forth for what felt like a very long time, Arimay finally began to show some improvement. She was anticipating Vanessa's moves rather than reacting the same way each time. *Of course, she reacts by moving away instead of blocking me with her own weapon,* Vanessa thought. *But I'll take what I can get.*

"Are you sure you don't want to spend some extra quality time with Danilo tomorrow morning?" Vanessa teased.

"Never!" Arimay let out a battle cry as she stepped away from Vanessa's attack and brought her sword to her mentor's arm.

"Nice work."

"So you've like, actually fought in battles doing this?" Arimay gasped as she knelt and caught her breath. "And not been completely exhausted after five minutes?"

"Yes. Well, often more complicated techniques than these are required in those situations. But our swords from Aric are made from the best materials around. If you learn how to use them right, you will hardly ever wish for a different weapon."

"Good to know."

"I'll give this one to you, Arimay," Vanessa said as she sat down and signaled the end of the pretend fight. "You did very well. We'll end our training here for today."

Upon hearing those words Arimay dramatically collapsed onto the ground, pretending to be asleep.

* * *

After a week of repeating the same exercises in an attempt to get Arimay more comfortable with Danilo, Alexander decided to try something different.

"Today we will ride out to the Meadow of Sunlight," he explained. "It's about a half-hour's journey from here and it will give you more of an opportunity to bond with your horse."

"*Bond* with my horse?" Arimay stared at Alexander as if he had grown a second head.

"I know you and Danilo didn't get off to a great start," Vanessa said, "but you need to give him a chance. He doesn't know you very well either. As you spend more time with him, he will become more relaxed around you."

Arimay nodded and let her mentors lead the way.

When they reached the edge of the meadow they slowed their horses to a stop. Arimay stared at the bright array of wildflowers with her mouth gaping open.

"I grew up so close to this place," she said, "but I've never seen it before. It's so beautiful."

"It sure is," Vanessa replied. "This was the first place

in Adhiren that I ever saw, and I felt that way too. It was more like home than anywhere else. The place I used to live wasn't as beautiful as this."

"You mean the village in the forest? I've heard some stories about what you did. Not many though, as they are technically forbidden in my city."

"What happens if someone gets caught telling stories about King Aric and his army in your city?"

Arimay shrugged. "I'm not sure. I think it depends on how often a person is reported to be doing so. The first time, they get a stern warning from a government official. Then public humiliation. Some people have even been sent to jail."

"So how did you hear about Aric then?"

Arimay sighed and closed her eyes. "My Uncle Jedrin. I used to stay with him sometimes when I was little. He ran into some people under Malik's influence on a sea voyage that was part of Galemoor's mission to explore the island of Ust'Naran. There was a Dove that came to his aid, and told him about King Aric. He used to tell me stories late at night when my Aunt had fallen asleep. He made me promise not to tell anyone. My mother and I, we were servants for the Galemoorian upper class. When a group of diplomats requested additional help on their trip to Emeraldia, I begged her to let me go with them. I told her I wanted to see more of the world, but really I wanted to see if the stories about Aric were true. She wasn't very fond of the idea, but finally she agreed to let me go."

Arimay paused. "I may never see her again."

"I'm so sorry."

An awkward silence hung between Arimay and Vanessa for quite some time and Vanessa didn't know what to say. She had so many questions: *Does her family know where she is? What did she have to go through to get here? I want to ask her, but if I ask too many questions she might feel overwhelmed and might not trust me. I can't let that happen. I'll just have to wait.*

Alexander broke the silence when he saw that the sun was beginning to cast a dark orange hue over the meadow.

"We should head back soon. But before we do, would you like to try one of the best rubiberries in the entire country?"

Arimay gave him a timid smile. Vanessa turned Shadow around and led her, with Arimay following, to the same berry bushes she and Brianna had eaten from during her first day in Adhiren. Alexander picked some of the biggest, juiciest berries and handed them to Vanessa and Arimay. As beautiful as the moment was, Vanessa couldn't help but think that soon the sun would set and she would be back in the dark in more ways than one.

CHAPTER SIX

"NO, HELENA. YOU CAN'T!"

Vanessa knelt beside her oldest and dearest friend. She could hardly see through the tears that were streaming down her face. Helena was lying very still in her bed, covered by a thin blanket. She was struggling to breathe. The doctor stood beside them shaking his head.

"Vani," Helena spoke with a raspy voice. "I am old, and I am very sick. This is a natural part of life, you know."

"But I don't want to live without you. You can't leave yet; I'm not ready."

"If the High King has decided it is time for me to join his kingdom," Helena gasped as she drew in another weak breath, "who am I to refuse?"

"Oh Helena." The tears were impossible to stop. Vanessa gripped Helena's hand tightly. Then she heard a terrible sound that sent chills down her spine. Everything went dark as a cold breeze whipped around the room. Then a creature with a vague human form emerged. It was made of the same billowing smoke as the creature at her door had been the week before. It carried a spear made of fire that matched its thin, slanted eyes. It hissed as it stared at Vanessa. Then it turned to Helena.

"No!" Vanessa screamed, reaching out to protect her friend. But it was too late. The creature attacked Helena with the spear, and she let out her last breath. She was gone.

With a start, Vanessa opened her eyes. She was shaking uncontrollably and trying to slow her breathing. She noticed the same shadowy creature lounging against her bedroom wall, arms folded across its chest with a smug smile on its face.

"You," she growled, pointing at the creature. "You killed my friend!" She lunged out of bed and grabbed a lit torch from its place on the wall. She swung it a couple of times, but it did not seem to cause the creature any pain. The weapon went right through it. The creature watched her pathetic attempts to try and destroy it, laughing eerily and shaking its head as if Vanessa were a weak child who was pretending to be fierce and strong.

Once Vanessa realized her attempts were futile, she lowered her torch. "Go away," she said through gritted teeth. She held her stance should the creature decide to attack.

"I have an offer for you," the creature hissed. "From my great and powerful king."

"Why would I make a deal with you?"

"Because I can take away your nightmares."

Vanessa stared at the creature curiously.

"I can ensure you have pleasant dreams for the rest of

your life. No more replaying that scene with Naara. No more painful reminders of your dead friends that you failed to save."

Her eyes widened. "How can you do that? And how do you know about Naara and the others?"

"My king has eyes all over this world. He has seen your bravery and your sacrifice. He needs committed fighters like yourself and wishes to help end your suffering."

Vanessa's heart skipped a beat. *I've been so much weaker since the nightmares started. Some people think I'm going crazy. Even I think I'm going crazy! I can't keep up my image as a strong, confident soldier much longer. And now I have to set a good example for Arimay. This creature says it can help me. But at what price will the deal come?*

"Explain. What exactly are you offering?" she asked the creature, pointing her torch at it.

"If you swear allegiance to my king," it said, "he can use his power to take away your nightmares. Not only that, but he can help you to become stronger and more confident in your fighting skills. You can become the soldier you deserve to be, the one that everyone thinks you already are."

"What do I have to give up in order for your king to do this?"

"Nothing, except your allegiance to King Aric."

Vanessa took a step back. "Why would I do that?"

"Aric and his father are very powerful. So are the Doves. Why have they not taken the nightmares away from you? Why have they not made you stronger?"

"I...I don't know."

"Think about it," the creature encouraged. "He wants to keep all the power and honour for himself."

"Vanessa!" Alexander's voice cut through the trancelike state Vanessa had found herself in while speaking with the creature. Her father ran into the room, sword in hand. The sword was glowing almost as brightly as the moon.

"Leave," he pointed the sword at the creature. "Leave my daughter and my house alone."

The creature covered its face in an attempt to hide from the light. It let out a hiss and then vanished.

"Are you alright?" Alexander ran to his daughter. "What happened? Why didn't you call for help?"

"I....I don't....it killed Helena, dad."

"What are you talking about?"

"She was already sick and dying, but then that monster showed up and *murdered* her. I didn't even get to say a proper goodbye." She began to cry.

"Vanessa, honey," Alexander took his daughter into his arms. "Helena isn't dead. That was a dream."

Vanessa wiped her eyes and looked up at her father. "Really?" she gasped.

"Yes, really. And she isn't sick either. You saw her on your way home from Emeraldia the other day. Remember?"

Vanessa took a step away from her father as her reality became clear once again.

"It said it could take away my nightmares."

"Oh?"

"It said if I gave up my allegiance to Aric it would

make me stronger."

"And do you believe that?"

"Of course not. Not now that the vile thing is out of my head. But why won't Aric help with the nightmares?"

Alexander shook his head. "I don't know," he replied. He turned to look out the window. "The Doves are here," he pointed to the two white birds who were watching them. "We don't need to worry about that shadow creature anymore."

Vanessa sighed. "Okay. Thanks for getting rid of him."

"I would do anything for you," Alexander kissed his daughter's head. "Now try and get some sleep."

"Okay. Goodnight, dad." Vanessa pulled the sheets back around her shoulders and tried to think of peaceful things as the Doves kept watch.

* * *

As Vanessa met the gaze of other soldiers huddled on the Emera Fields the next morning she knew she was not the only one who had met a strange visitor in the night. Everyone was talking in hushed tones. Many were shaking and she was certain it wasn't due to the chill in the air. They all had dark circles under their eyes.

A few people kept glancing behind them, weapons at the ready, as if expecting an attack. Almost all of them were struggling to keep their eyes open.

Vanessa saw the king and approached him with a bow. "Your Majesty," she began, "I need to talk to you about…"

Aric placed a hand on her shoulder. "I know, Vanessa. I know. The Doves told me everything. I must speak with all of you immediately."

A trumpet blast caused the entire army to turn their attention to Aric. Vanessa walked over to Brianna and put her head on her shoulder. Without saying a word, Brianna wrapped her in a warm embrace.

"My dear people," the voice of King Aric rang out across the fields. "I was hoping to never have to speak with you about what I must discuss today. The Doves and I have been monitoring the situation for awhile now and I fear you are all in grave danger. Malik has infiltrated our ranks…"

Gasps came from the crowd.

"…but he has not invaded in the way that so many of us expected and have been training for. Instead of a physical attack, it appears he is trying to weaken you by attacking your minds. Malik now possesses the ability to access your thoughts. What terrible power allowed him to do so I do not even want to think about. The Doves have observed that he has created terrible shadow creatures that obey his every command. They have been visiting many of your homes under the cover of darkness, while you are asleep. They lie in wait for you to wake up from a nightmare, and then attempt to strike more fear into your hearts. They offer you something your heart greatly desires, in order to convince you to leave

Adhiren with them and fight for Malik instead. They are able to hold a hypnotic sort of trance on their victims. Already it has been reported that five of our soldiers have fallen for this tactic and disappeared in the middle of the night. This display of such terrible power is frightening indeed."

Nods of agreement came from many of the soldiers, including Vanessa.

"The Doves have reported their presence over the past few days, but we still don't know their numbers or Malik's full intent in unleashing them. All we know right now is that light seems to weaken them and make them disappear. The most effective light comes from the swords you all received when you joined my army."

Gasps of shock came from the crowd as they reached for the pommels of their finely ornamented weapons.

"As some of you have discovered in the past few days," Aric continued, "your swords will give off a bright white light as hot as fire in the presence of a Shadow Walker. It will not harm you in any way, but any Shadow Walker that looks at it or is close to it will feel great pain and distress. The Doves have observed that drawing these specific swords around the creatures weakens their power. I would advise all of you to keep torches lit in and around your homes at all times. Make sure you are never alone, especially at night. Keep your swords close. Surround yourself with fellow soldiers for extra support and protection. You will be harder to fool if someone is able to help you fight them off and remind you of the truth of how terrible Malik is. The Doves will also be on patrol in increased numbers. Training is cancelled for today. Go home and get some rest while I speak with my father about these Shadow Walkers. I want all of you to meet back here first thing tomorrow morning, and every morning. We will do a roll call and share what else we have learned."

"Yes, King Aric," one soldier replied, raising his sword to show support. "Long live the king!" The rest of Aric's Army followed suit. Aric nodded, showing his appreciation of the gesture, and then dismissed them.

Vanessa and Brianna walked side-by-side as they headed back to Kalmehara.

"So you haven't had nightmares, or seen one of these horrible creatures?" Vanessa asked.

"No," Brianna replied. "But Aiyanna has. She started having bad dreams a few nights ago, which is strange because she never used to have them. She was never scared of having a monster under her bed or anything like that. Now she really *is* seeing a monster. I wish I could take the nightmares away from her, but I can't. The most I can do is help to chase the Shadow Walkers away when they come."

"I hope Aric and his father figure out how to get rid of them soon. I can't take much more of this."

Brianna turned to face Vanessa. "No matter what happens, I'll always be here for you, okay? If you're scared, tired, need to cry, whatever, you can tell me. You don't have to be 'Vanessa the Brave Hero' in front of me if you don't want to be."

"Thanks, Brianna." Vanessa gave her friend a hug.

"And same goes for you okay? If you're scared or stressed you can always come talk to me about it. My dad's a great listener too."

"Deal." The two friends shook hands as if creating a serious, binding contract. Then they parted ways and went home with their families to prepare for the challenges ahead.

CHAPTER SEVEN

"VANESSA, BRING ME SOME flour will you?" Alexander asked. He was busy pounding dough on the counter with his bare hands.

"Here you go," Vanessa replied, dumping a small cup of flour over her father's work surface.

"Thanks." He began to roll out the dough with a rolling pin.

"I think you forgot something," Vanessa said with a smirk.

"What's that?"

Vanessa grabbed a bowl full of diced pears from the other end of the table and set them before her father.

"Oh dear." Alexander sighed, wiping his brow with a floury hand. "How could I have forgotten one of the most important things?" He grabbed the pears, dumped them on the table and began to work them into the dough.

"Everyone's been a little stressed lately," Vanessa reassured her father. "Oh, and you have flour in your hair."

"Where?" Alexander raised his hand to feel the top of

his head.

"Well, it's all over you now." she grabbed a pinch of flour and flicked it at him. Some of it landed in his beard.

In response Alexander slammed his hand on the flour-filled table with a smirk. Then he reached for Vanessa and held onto her with one hand. He used his other one to wipe flour all over her face.

"Blegh!" she exclaimed. She laughed as she tried to wipe it off. "I guess we're going to have to wash all of this off later. And maybe clean the kitchen." Their horsing around had covered almost the entire kitchen in white powder.

Alexander shrugged as he wiped his hands on his shirt. "It will give me something to do while I wait for my patrol shift later tonight."

As the Pinnamari bread was baking over the fire, Vanessa and her father made preparations to protect themselves from the Shadow Walkers. They lit torches around the house and barricaded the front door with furniture. They closed the shutters and boarded them up, except for one to allow the Doves in and out. They placed their swords from Aric near their beds, as well as extra torches in case they needed them. They set out clothing they would need for the next day. Then they sat down and enjoyed some of their warm, freshly baked treat.

There was a knock at the door. Vanessa ran to stick her head out their only open window. Aiyanna and Jahzara, Brianna's younger sisters, were standing there. They looked confused by Vanessa's appearance in the window instead of the doorway.

"We barricaded the door to protect against the Shadow Walkers," Vanessa explained.

"Good idea!" Jahzara said. The blue flower crown on her head shifted slightly and she adjusted it to keep it out of her eyes.

"Vanessa," Aiyanna asked, "will you come and dance with us? One of the soldiers on patrol on our street is playing his flute and another brought their fiddle. Mama and Papa said we could stay out for a bit and join them if you and Brianna are with us." The little girls jumped up and down with excitement. Their bright blue eyes shone with anticipation. It had been many days since they were allowed out of the house in the evening.

"Sure," Vanessa replied with a smile. "I'm going to have to crawl out this window though."

The smell of freshly baked Pinnamari bread wafted on the evening breeze. Jahzara's blue eyes widened. "Is that Pinnamari bread? Can I have some?"

Vanessa laughed. "Of course. I will bring some for Brianna and your other friends too."

"Yay!" the little girls both cheered. Vanessa climbed through the window with the freshly baked treats and went to join in the celebrations. Aiyanna and Jahzara eagerly reached for the bread and then ran ahead of Vanessa to where a small crowd was gathering to sing and dance.

The sweet, airy sounds of the flute and fiddle wafted into the early evening air, complemented by the flickering lights of fireflies and the glow of the sunset. Brianna had also made a flower crown and was distributing more to the younger children as they gathered. The soldier playing the fiddle, named Faylon, had composed a song to lighten the spirits of the weary soldiers who had been working so many long nights. He sang for the group as they danced:

In the shadows of the night
When terror comes to steal the light
We will raise our swords with a mighty yell
Courage, courage, all is well!
Courage, courage, all is well!
Malik wants to feed your fear
But Aric and Doves are always near
His power we to the creatures tell
Courage, courage, all is well!
Courage, courage, all is well!

Vanessa returned home, exhausted but happy, moments before her father left for the first patrol of the night. He let her in the door and she locked it behind him. She settled into bed, confident that no nightmares would be coming for her this time.

All was quiet and calm until a rustling sound startled Vanessa awake. When she opened her eyes she saw a shadow standing in her doorway. This time it looked like an actual human and not a Shadow Walker, but she grabbed her sword just in case. It was glowing slightly, but not as intensely as Aric had described earlier.

"Dad, is that you?" she whispered, in case her eyes were deceiving her again.

"No," the voice spoke. She knew that voice. She knew it so well.

"Jareth?" She hopped out of bed and lit a torch so she could see his face.

Jareth stepped into the light and Vanessa gasped. His short black hair, which he usually kept tidy, was so messy she guessed it hadn't been brushed in at least a week. He was dirty, and badly bruised. He had a long cut running down the side of his face. It looked fresh.

"It's so good to see you." She stepped forward to embrace Jareth, but stopped short. There was something in his eyes that made her uneasy. She took a step back. "I…we've all been so worried."

"I am fine," Jareth replied in a monotone, although his appearance seemed to contradict the statement.

"Where have you been?"

"A far better place than here."

Vanessa tilted her head curiously. *What place could be better than Adhiren?*

"But you're back now, right?"

"Why would I want to stay?" Jareth asked.

"Why are you here if you didn't want to come back?"

"To convince you to come with me."

"Where are you going?"

"Back to Tar'Máran."

Silence hung in the air for a few moments as Vanessa processed what had happened.

"So the Shadow Walkers *did* take you."

"No, they didn't take me." Jareth shook his head. "I went with them on my own."

"Why? What did they offer you?"

"An esteemed place in Malik's army."

"Why would you even…"

Jareth sighed and rolled his eyes. He folded his arms across his chest as he addressed his old friend. "You don't understand, Vanessa. You have everything. Your family is all here with you in Adhiren, happy, healthy and alive. You're one of the most popular soldiers in Aric's Army, and dare I say one of Aric's favourites. I am not popular; the other soldiers make fun of me. I have no family. They died in Leftrock Village. They burned to death…"

"But Malik is the one who…"

"…no one in Aric's Army will ever look up to me or respect me like they do you. There's no point in me sticking around here. I have found where I belong."

"Jareth, I don't have everything," Vanessa said, desperately trying to convince her friend to change his mind. "My life isn't perfect. Not everyone looks up to me, but I really don't think I'm worthy of respect from the ones that do. I've lost people too. But I know that Tar'Máran is not where we belong. Please stay here. Talk to Aric. He's going to fix this."

Jareth shook his head. "You are one of my oldest friends, Vanessa. I care about you. I only want what's best for you. You need to stop believing that Aric can fix everything when clearly he can't. If he could, he would have done so when the first person went missing. You're being naïve. Just come with me. The Shadow Walkers really aren't so bad. They want to help us. You'll see." He held an outstretched hand toward Vanessa.

"No." she replied firmly.

"That's what Naara said too," Jareth replied grimly. "And then she died." He pulled his hand down and glared at Vanessa. The look reminded her of the one Malik gave her when she was a prisoner in his palace years before.

"Jareth, stop." She pleaded as a tear ran down her face. "Don't bring Naara into this. That was different."

"Aric didn't care about her either."

"That's not true."

"Then why did he leave her to die?"

"I don't know."

"Join me," Jareth hissed.

"No," Vanessa replied.

"Fine." Jareth pulled out a dagger from his pocket and pointed it at Vanessa. "I tried to do this the easy way. But my Master did warn me I might have to use force." He lunged forward, but Vanessa was ready. She blocked the blow and began to inch backward toward her window.

Jareth swung at her head and she ducked with a scream. Jumping up, Vanessa grabbed his arm and tried to take the dagger. As they both struggled she could see Jareth's face turning red.

"You don't want to do this," she said.

Jareth turned away and yanked his arm from her grip. He spun around, grabbed a handful of Vanessa's hair and kneed her in the stomach. "If you do not support me in this, Vanessa, you are no longer my friend."

Gasping for breath, Vanessa stood up and swung her

arm toward Jareth. She hit him square in the face and he took a couple of steps back, giving his head a shake before coming at her again. He swung for her head but she caught his arm and pulled him down.

"I will always fight for King Aric," she said.

"Fool." Jareth's dagger cut through one of the sleeves of Vanessa's nightdress. She winced at the pain as blood began to seep through the clothing, but knew that the fight wasn't over. The look in Jareth's eyes said that he was fighting to kill. She charged at him with her sword and he blocked the blow, just barely. Her heart was pounding so loudly she was sure the neighbours could hear it.

If nothing else, Jareth's fighting skills had greatly improved since he had left Adhiren. He was almost better than Vanessa. *Almost, but not quite.*

By now Jareth had his former friend backed up against a boarded-up window. Vanessa tried to sneak under his arms and move away from the wall but he blocked her every time. *I have nowhere else to go. I can't hold out much longer. He has me cornered. What am I supposed to do?*

"Doves!" she cried as she continued to duck and dodge blows as best she could. "Please help!"

"Your little bird friends aren't coming," Jareth hissed. But he was about to be proven wrong.

A welcome noise of twittering birds soon filled the room. Two Doves flew in through the open window in the living room and began to peck at Jareth's face. With a surprised yelp he dropped the dagger and ran for the closest window. He punched a hole through the boards and jumped out into the night, not looking back even once.

"Thank you," Vanessa sighed as she collapsed on the floor.

"You are most welcome," the first Dove replied. Then it perked up and looked around as if hearing something only they could hear. "I fear tonight's battles are not yet over. We must be off, but you need to see to your father."

My father? It was strange that he hadn't woken up during her fight with Jareth. *Right. He was on patrol tonight. He must have just gotten home.*

As the Doves flew away she heard the faintest whisper coming from down the hall: "I really could see her again? You have no idea what that would mean to me."

Glowing sword in hand, Vanessa jumped up and ran to the living room. Her father was awake, standing up and talking to a Shadow Walker. Vanessa's sword shone as bright as the sun.

"Yes, we can arrange a meeting with your dear wife," it hissed, "but it will come at a cost, of course." It held out a hand to her father.

Alexander did not even hear his daughter enter the room. He was entranced by the foul creature and its offer. He reached up to grab its hand.

"Go away!" Vanessa yelled, flinging the sword in its face. "You are not welcome here."

The creature shrieked and pulled back its hand. Then it vanished, leaving Alexander to collapse onto the floor.

"Father," Vanessa said, bending down and holding onto his head. "Are you alright?"

With a groan, Alexander blinked slowly and looked up at his daughter.

"What happened?"

"Shadow Walker. It said it could take you to see Sarah."

"Oh dear," he sat up, rubbing his forehead. "I don't know what I was thinking."

"It wasn't your fault, Dad. The Shadow Walkers are very powerful. I'm glad I didn't lose you tonight." She gave her father a hug. "I saw Jareth."

"What?" Alexander pulled away from his daughter's embrace and held her at arm's length. He saw the wound on her arm. "Did he hurt you?"

"He snuck into our house, while you were sleeping." Vanessa said in a rushed tone, as if needing to get the entire explanation out in a single breath. "He said he went willingly with the Shadow Walkers and is now trying to recruit more soldiers for them. He tried to kill me because I wouldn't go with him but the Doves helped chase him off."

Alexander held his daughter close. "This is more serious than I thought."

"More serious than any of us thought."

"From now on, we will both sleep here in the living room," her father declared, "and we will have torches and weapons at the ready. I lost you once, and I'm not going to lose you again."

* * *

At the meeting the next morning it seemed as if the entire Army of Aric was trembling in fear. The bright sun and presence of their king couldn't quite shake off what they had experienced in the night.

Brianna saw the look in Vanessa's eyes and knew right away that something was wrong. "What happened last night?" she asked in a grim tone.

"I saw Jareth."

"Really? Did he tell you where he's been?"

"He's with the Shadow Walkers now. He tried to kill me."

Brianna gasped. "That's horrible, I'm so sorry."

"And then once he left I had to save my father from a Shadow Walker. I almost lost him last night." Vanessa sighed and collapsed into her friend's embrace. "How were things at your house?"

"Aiyanna had another nightmare. A Shadow Walker came, but I was right there in the room with her so I chased it off pretty quickly."

Vanessa stood back up. "Where's Aric? He should be here by now."

"I'm sure he'll be here any minute."

Vanessa spotted her timid apprentice walking over to join them.

"A Shadow Walker took someone in the house next to me last night," she stated grimly. "We never had

Shadow Walkers in Galemoor."

"We've never had them here before either," Vanessa replied. "It's a new challenge and no one has quite figured out how to deal with them yet."

"What do you think King Aric is going to do?" Arimay asked.

"I don't know." Vanessa sighed. She wished she had a confident answer for the young apprentice, but after the past few days she was beginning to doubt that much could be done about their unwelcome guests at all.

After taking attendance of those present, it was determined that two more soldiers from Emeraldia and one from Kalmehara were missing, on top of the five that had disappeared the previous day. Aric asked if anyone had encountered the Shadow Walkers in the night and Vanessa found out that three other soldiers had similar visits from missing friends or family members, often accompanied by the vile creatures.

"It would seem that Malik has begun using his new prisoners to recruit more soldiers for his army," Aric commented. "This breaks my heart more than you will ever know."

The fields grew silent. No one knew what to say.

"What are we going to do about it?" one soldier asked.

"My father and I will be discussing that further today," Aric replied. "He will be making daily visits to the Emerald Palace from now on, until we figure out how to defeat the Shadow Walkers. I will be increasing the number of soldiers on guard duty around the palace and also around all of your homes. I will need each of you to take turns keeping your streets safe, keeping torches lit and alerting the Doves at once of any danger. The worst thing any of us can do right now is isolate ourselves. When you are alone, you do not recognize the lies being told to you as lies. The Shadow Walkers can manipulate you to believe whatever they want you to believe. That is how they lead you away to Malik. Remember that, and stay together."

"Yes, my king," the soldier who had previously spoken out replied. The rest of Aric's Army bowed to their leader, acknowledging their understanding of his command.

"I want you to spend one hour practicing one-on-one attacks and defenses, and quick responses to the presence of Shadow Walkers. After that you may be dismissed. Those who are not on guard duty immediately should get some rest."

The crowd began to split up, but Arimay stayed by Vanessa's side.

"Vanessa, can I ask you something?"

"Of course."

"Can I stay with you? Juwan and Seth are always off somewhere together, and the grown-ups aren't in the houses very often. Other people have their families to look after them but I..." there was a slight hitch in her voice as she continued, "I don't want to be alone if the Shadow Walkers come."

Vanessa tried her best to hide her discomfort at this request. She wanted Arimay to feel safe and was partially responsible for her, but letting her into her home would mean she would know about her nightmare problem, and that she wasn't always as strong and brave as everybody thought. *Everyone is having nightmares now,* she told herself, *so she won't know the difference.* The fact didn't do much to ease her upset stomach as she closed her eyes, took a deep breath and said, "Of course you can. My father and I would be happy to have you."

Vanessa and her father led Arimay back to their home in Kalmehara. She gasped in awe as she looked around the four-room house.

"It's so beautiful," she whispered as she ran her hand across the wooden kitchen table. Vanessa had never considered home to be beautiful. It was pretty small and unfurnished compared to some of the other families' places on their street. *But compared to Arimay's previous circumstances, it must feel like a palace.*

Arimay eyed the Pinnamari bread eagerly and Alexander offered her a piece. Her eyes widened in amazement as she bit into the sweet treat.

"I've never had this before," she exclaimed with her mouth full, "but I like it!" Vanessa then gave Arimay a quick tour of the neighborhood. She introduced her to Brianna's sisters Aiyanna and Jahzara and showed her the horses in the stable where her father worked. They returned home to prepare supper while Alexander finished tending to the horses. After dinner the three of them gathered supplies for torches and anything they could use as weapons against Malik's newest minions. They set up three mats with blankets in the living room. As Vanessa and Arimay set their special swords near their pillows and prepared to go to sleep, Alexander went out the front door. He was on the first patrol shift for their street that night. Vanessa locked the door behind him and turned to her guest.

"Do you need anything else?" she asked Arimay.

"No, I'm okay." The young girl covered her head with a blanket and was soon fast asleep.

Vanessa laid down and tried not to panic. *Not tonight,* she pleaded. *Please, no nightmares tonight.*

CHAPTER EIGHT

IT WAS DARK AND the air reeked of smoke. Vanessa coughed as she pulled part of her cloak up over her face. She could hear wails and screams of people in pain echoing in the darkness. Then she heard a terrible thumping noise that shook the ground beneath her. She tried to maintain her balance but almost fell over. She looked up to see a Shadow Walker the size of a large building stomping through the street. It laughed maniacally as it lashed its flaming whips at its unsuspecting victims. There were all sorts of people running down the street trying to escape certain death: soldiers in Aric's Army, people from Gal'Mesh, Naara, and even the little boy from Madejia that she met during her brief visit to the Kingdom of the Sky. The vile creature was setting houses on fire, destroying everything and everyone in its wake.

"Vanessa!" a familiar voice called. It was her father. He was in the path of the Shadow Walker and running as fast as his legs could take him. All around him horses ran down the street as they whinnied in fear. *He released them from the stable to try and save them. Always thinking of others before himself, even the animals.*

"Run," he panted. "I'll catch up to you."

"No. I'm waiting for you. I won't leave without you!"

The Shadow Walker turned and glared at Vanessa. It slunk ever closer to where her father was. Before she could blink, a fiery whip had wrapped around Alexander's leg and tripped him, sending him plummeting to the ground.

"No!" Vanessa screamed. "I won't let you do this."

The creature let out an unsettling laugh. "You can't stop me. I will take away everything and everyone you love."

She tried to run toward her father but some unseen force kept her frozen in place. With one swift movement the Shadow Walker stomped on her father and he was gone.

"No!" Vanessa collapsed to the ground weeping. She heard another eerie laugh and looked up to see the creature extending her a billowing hand.

"This will be your reality," it hissed. "Unless you join me and my Master."

"I will never do that," she replied. "This isn't my life. This can't be my life. Aric, he's going to save us, I…"

A painful burning sensation coursed through her body as the Shadow Walker's whip ripped through her skin. She let out a scream.

"Vanessa?" a timid voice called out. *Who is that?* Vanessa woke with a start to see Arimay leaning over her. As her vision became less blurry she could tell that Arimay had been crying. The poor girl looked like a baby animal who had narrowly escaped the jaws of a hungry predator.

Vanessa rubbed her eyes and blinked as a sudden realization set in. It had been a week since Arimay had been staying with Vanessa and her father. There hadn't been any nightmares in that time and she had hoped they had disappeared for good. *No such luck.*

She groaned. *Arimay knows now. I tried to hide it from her but she knows.*

"Are you okay?"

I have to do this.

"I had a nightmare."

"That seemed a lot scarier than regular nightmares."

"It was."

"How?"

Vanessa took a deep breath. "There's a lot you don't know about me, Arimay."

"Like what?"

Silence hung in the air as she gathered the courage to continue speaking. "Two years ago, on the way back to Adhiren, I lost a friend. Her name was Naara. She would be about your age now. She was funny, smart, and liked to wear flowers in her hair. She was the best storyteller I've ever met."

"She sounds nice."

"She was." A tear ran down Vanessa's face. "I told her about what Malik was going to do to the forest, and how Aric could help us, but she wouldn't listen. I begged and pleaded with her and she still chose not to come with me. I'm not sure if she made it out alive, Arimay. Her whole village burnt down. And many people died in my own village. I couldn't save everyone and it haunts me every day. I try to be happy around the other soldiers and their children, but inside I feel like I'm going to fall apart. I've had nightmares for years but the Shadow Walkers are making things worse. Soon I fear that I won't have any strength left. I worry that everyone I love is going to die and I won't be able to help them. I'm so sorry I'm not doing a good job of being your mentor. Everything is falling apart and I don't know what to do anymore. I don't know if I can be good at anything."

Arimay put a hand on her mentor's shoulder. "It's okay," she said. "I've had nightmares before too. I was starting to think you might actually *be* perfect," she let out an awkward chuckle, "but now that you've told me this, I know you're a normal person like me. And that's not a bad thing. You have helped me a lot. I want to help you if I can. I know what it's like to feel alone and scared and it's not fun at all."

Arimay embraced Vanessa and held her until her tears subsided. "You have taught me so much already. Together we can keep the Shadow Walkers away from this house."

A loud bugle blast sounded nearby as Vanessa pulled away from Arimay's embrace.

"Shadow Walkers."

"They're here."

"Let's go."

Vanessa and Arimay picked up their swords and burst out the front door with them drawn and ready to fight. Other soldiers came pouring out of their houses as well, converging at the scene of the attack. Dark, billowing smoke was rising from a few of the houses. From one they could hear a baby crying. In another, a man saying, "I'll do whatever you want. Take me to him!"

Vanessa and Arimay charged into one of the houses, along with Alexander and a couple other soldiers. Brightly-lit swords drawn, they converged in a bedroom where four Shadow Walkers had surrounded a young man and his wife. The man was on his knees, begging and pleading with a smug-looking Shadow Walker. Tears were streaming down his face as he trembled before the vile creature.

"Please, show me where my son is. I will go with you if you can take me to him."

One of the soldiers coughed. The man turned around and gasped, shocked to find so many strangers in his house at such a late hour. His wife had crawled behind the bed in an attempt to hide from the Shadow Walkers.

"It's okay," the man said with a dazed expression. "We were just talking. It's seen my son. It can take me to him."

"It is *not* okay," Vanessa replied, glaring at the monster.

"You are not welcome here," Alexander added, pointing his glowing weapon at another one of the beasts.

"By the order of King Aric you must leave at once!" another soldier cried, jabbing their sword through the middle of another Shadow Walker.

A battle cry rose up from the small group. The creatures shrieked and covered their ears as if the noise was too much for them. Within moments they had vanished and the man collapsed in exhaustion.

The woman crawled back out from behind the bed and sat beside her husband. "Is he going to be okay?" she asked. Her face was red, puffy and covered in tear stains, and she was still shaking.

"He should be," Vanessa reassured her. "Just give him a couple of minutes."

After a few moments the man who had been talking to the Shadow Walker came back to his senses. Deprived of most of his strength, he turned to face his wife. She supported his head in her hands and they both began to cry.

"It said it saw Ben," he sobbed. "It said we could see him again. That we could bring him home."

"Oh Jason," the woman sighed. "Ben is dead. The Shadow Walkers got him a week ago. We saw it happen."

The couple embraced and cried together for quite some time, overwhelmed by intense pain that came from losing their child and the realization of what could have happened to them that night.

"Do you have your swords?" Alexander asked as his group prepared to leave to give the couple some privacy.

"Yes," the woman wiped her eyes and looked up at Alexander. "They're in the other room."

"Keep them close at all times," Alexander advised. "And keep a few additional torches lit around your home."

"Thank you for helping us," the woman said. "If it weren't for you I would have lost my husband tonight."

"It is an honour to serve fellow members of Aric's Army," Alexander replied with a nod. "There are guards on patrol throughout the night if you should need anything else." He led Vanessa, Arimay, and the rest of the group out of the house. They leaned up against a wall and caught their breath.

"I don't think," Arimay gasped, "I will ever get used to this."

"I hope you don't have to," Vanessa replied. "Things weren't always like this in Adhiren. We had peace before the Shadow Walkers came. Aric says he and his father are working on a plan to eliminate these foul creatures once and for all. I hope he plans on putting it into action soon."

Vanessa and Arimay both fell asleep sitting up, leaning up against the wall of the house. Alexander woke them up later that night and brought them back to their home.

* * *

The following weeks held a similar routine: rest during the day, take patrol shifts, and chase off Shadow Walkers at night. Regular training had been put off until further notice. Vanessa and Dillan did their best to plan their schedules so they could visit each other at least once a week, but it was not easy with all the responsibilities they had. She hadn't seen Gaerwin, Nimeesha, or many of her other friends for a long time. Arimay was becoming more confident and would occasionally dismiss the Shadow Walkers herself, with her sword raised and a commanding tone. Often Vanessa, her father and the rest of the soldiers on her street were able to chase away their enemies with little resistance.

Not all of the attempts to chase away Malik's minions were successful however. Some soldiers who had not attended the meetings where Aric explained how to fight the Shadow Walkers ran at them with sticks and regular swords, and were promptly eaten by the beasts to the horror of those watching from the relative safety of their homes. Arimay and Vanessa stuck close together, especially when the terrible creatures roamed the streets at night. No Shadow Walkers had made an appearance in their own house in a while, and the possibility of an unwelcome guest was barely on Vanessa's mind as she drifted off to sleep.

* * *

A bloodcurdling scream pierced through Vanessa's consciousness in the middle of the night. With a sharp breath she sat up and looked around. Arimay was thrashing around in her sleep, tossing blankets everywhere. A Shadow Walker was lurking in the corner of the room bearing a grim smile.

"Arimay!" Vanessa cried as she put her hands on the girl's shoulders. "Arimay wake up!"

"Huh?" Arimay sat up. "Don't hurt me Jadon," she pleaded, covering her face as a shadowy servant of Malik loomed over her. "I left you and the rest of the family alone. You can go back now. Let me be!"

A deep, unsettling laugh caused the young apprentice to look through her fingers at the monster. "Jadon? Where's Jadon?"

"He's not here," the Shadow Walker hissed. "For now. But I can't guarantee he won't come looking for you here. When he returns home he will not think twice about hurting your mother and sister to get information of your whereabouts."

"Don't hurt my family," Arimay begged. "Please."

"I can only keep you safe if you come with me," a billowing outstretched hand gestured to Arimay. "When Jadon finds out where you are, he will stop at nothing to punish you for what you did to your family. It is not safe for you to remain here."

Arimay reached out her hand toward the shadowy figure. "Can you really keep me safe from him?" The Shadow Walker tilted its head and gave her an eerie smile.

"No!" Vanessa cried, swatting her apprentice's hand away from the enemy. Arimay shrieked and fell backward, landing on the floor with a thud.

"You are not welcome here," Vanessa said to the Shadow Walker. She raised her glowing sword and held it in front of its face. "By order of King Aric you must leave at once!"

"Fine." the Shadow Walker shrugged. "But you should not have this girl in your home. She will only bring trouble and disgrace to you and your family. Isn't that right, Arimay?"

Arimay shuddered and huddled up with her arms around her legs. She refused to meet Vanessa's gaze.

With another eerie laugh, the horrible creature vanished. Vanessa rushed to her apprentice's side. Arimay was crying again.

"It was a dream," Vanessa told Arimay as she wrapped her arms around her apprentice. "It was a nightmare, Arimay. It can't hurt you."

Arimay turned to face her with more tears welling up in her eyes. "But how do you know? How can you know for sure?"

"Because that creature is a liar," Vanessa said. "It tried to lead you away to Malik but I wouldn't let it do that."

Arimay shook her head and rubbed her eyes. Slowly her breathing was beginning to return to normal. She flopped back onto her mat. "I'm so sorry Vanessa. I can't believe I almost fell for that." she sighed. "What would have happened to me…"

"Don't think about that," Vanessa reassured her. "You're safe. I'm here to help you, just as you've been here to help me. The Doves are watching, and people are patrolling the streets this very minute." She paused for a moment before asking, "Who's Jadon? Is he trying to hurt you?"

Arimay turned away from her mentor. "It's a long story."

"You need to tell someone," Vanessa said. "It doesn't

have to be me, but someone should know. You know what the Shadow Walkers are using to try and manipulate me. I can't always think clearly when they do that, and that's when you can help me. What if this happens again? You need someone to be able to understand so they can help you. If I hadn't been here tonight you could have been on your way to Tar'Máran by now."

CHAPTER NINE

ARIMAY SHUDDERED. She had been seconds away from becoming a slave of Malik because the Shadow Walker had known her deepest, darkest fears. Her heart sank as she continued to re-live her past with the words of warning ringing in her ears: "*He will not think twice about hurting your mother and sister to get information of your whereabouts.*" *Is it wrong to hope that he is dead?*

Vanessa sat next to her, glancing at the lit torches in the room while Arimay gathered her thoughts. *She's probably exhausted after fighting off that Shadow Walker for me. I always end up being a burden to people.*

As much as she hated to admit it, Arimay knew that her mentor was right. She needed to tell someone about Jadon and what had happened when she was younger. The memories still hurt as if they had happened yesterday. That's why the Shadow Walker was able to make it seem so real to her. *If it happens again, and no one knows why I am so scared, I could die. If I do tell someone, they may never look at me the same way again. They will not accept me like they do now. They will know that I am nothing but a burden. What should I do?*

A tiny shadow flickered in the open window. Its shape was familiar, and it wasn't menacing like the Shadow Walkers were. Arimay squinted her eyes to try and get a better look at the shape. It cocked its head to one side and let out a chirp. *A Dove!*

She met its gaze as the torch light from a soldier walking past the house lit up the window. Although no sound came from its mouth, Arimay was certain the bird was speaking to her. *Tell Vanessa,* it said. *It's alright. She will believe you.* Then the bird flew off into the night.

She turned back to face her mentor. Vanessa's reassuring smile calmed Arimay enough to believe that what the Dove had told her was true. She closed her eyes and took a deep breath. "Okay. I will tell you what happened. But please promise me you won't tell anyone else. I don't want the other people in Aric's Army making fun of me like they did back home."

"I promise." Vanessa held up her right hand. "And I won't make fun of you."

"In Galemoor, people look to the stars for knowledge," Arimay began. She pictured the royal officials of her city standing outside at night, pointing to maps and whispering to each other under the cover of darkness. She had seen it many times before.

"When a baby is born, they observe the stars that night to learn the child's purpose and their future. When I was born, the royal officials told my mother that the stars foretold I would be a great burden to my family and my city. My mother was upset and told them it wasn't my fault that I was born under those stars. She didn't believe their words, but many other people did. Especially since we were poor, and were seen as useless to many."

She closed her eyes and recalled people jeering at her and her mother in the marketplace, throwing rotten food at them and calling her a waste of space. A single tear ran down her cheek. "I never wanted anything other than to serve and be a helpful member of my city. I never hurt anyone. But my mother had publicly defied the prediction of the officials and I got very sick when I was young. That's when the mocking got worse."

"I'm so sorry," Vanessa's gentle voice replied. There was a look of genuine concern on her face.

"There were many months where I was unable to get out of bed. I could hardly even sit up to eat or drink. I was very weak and my mother feared I was going to die. None of the medicines from the local healer did any good, but my mother kept spending her money to try every possible solution. She and my siblings had to work extra hard because I wasn't able to help with any chores. My mother gave me most of her portions of food and water in the hopes that I would regain my strength. I felt so useless and there was nothing I could do about it."

Silence filled the room as she gathered her thoughts and willed herself to continue reliving the painful memories. *You have to tell her. Someone has to know. She hasn't kicked you out of her home so far...* Arimay gathered up her courage to continue speaking:

"My mother loved me even when I couldn't help the

family. That never changed. She always told me that one day I would do great things. And my little sister Maili would always sing songs and tell me stories to try and cheer me up. But my older brother Jadon began to resent me." She could still see it, a memory as clear as if it had happened yesterday. The hate in Jadon's dark-brown eyes the day he left the house and never returned. "He was the one in my nightmare. When I was sick, he told my mother that she was treating him and Maili as if they didn't exist. That she forgot they were working hard and hungry too. That they were actually doing something for the family and proving their worth. He told her she should let me die."

"I'm so sorry," Vanessa said, pulling Arimay into a gentle embrace. Arimay's tears were flowing faster now.

"He said that if my mother didn't give up on me and return her focus to her children who were actually useful in the family, he would kill me himself. My mother told him she wouldn't let that happen. She stood guard over me day and night and kept Maili with her. One night he came to my bedside with a knife in his hand, ready to end my life. He looked so angry; I'd never seen anyone look like that before. My mother and Maili were asleep beside me and I was too weak to call for help. I could barely move, let alone stand up and try to get out of his way. I started shaking and crying, sure that my life was about to end. He raised the knife and then suddenly stopped. There was a strange noise coming from outside the door. He turned and went outside to investigate and never returned."

"That's terrible," Vanessa said. "But I'm glad he didn't hurt you."

"I started to wonder if my family would be better off if I was dead. But in the morning I told my mother and sister what happened and they couldn't stop crying and hugging me. Things started to change when I was eight years old. My mother returned from the market one day saying that a generous man had offered to buy her some new medicine from a well-known healer who tended to the rich people of the city. He had heard about my illness and reassured her that the medicine would help me regain my strength. He did not laugh or mock her like the others, so she decided to trust him. The medicine tasted awful, like sour lemon and pine mixed together. I almost threw it up. I had to take it three times a day for a week. Soon I was able to help my mother more around the house and I didn't feel as useless anymore. The sickness never came back, but people would still mock me when they saw me in the streets. They would make jokes about how I was supposed to be dead. They spit at me and kicked dirt in my face. They said I had to work for my mother for the rest of my life to pay back everything she did for me. But my mother didn't see it that way. She wanted me to be free of the limits set on us by the government. If I ever found a way to do that, she said she would support me. So when I had the chance to come here, she made that happen. I wish she and my sister had been able to come too."

She was exhausted. The fear of Jadon coming back

to hurt her and the grief of losing contact with her mother and sister was almost too much to bear. She had never told her story aloud to anyone before. Remembering her mother's kindness was creating a sharp pain in her heart that she hadn't felt in a long time. "I miss her."

The two soldiers of Aric sat together in silence for awhile, sharing an embrace while Arimay tried to get her breathing back to normal. Having Vanessa there with her provided a comfort amidst the sorrow that she had never experienced before. As terrified as she had been to share her story, she also felt some relief that it was no longer a secret. *I hope she will keep her promise.*

"So...that's my story." She sniffled and wiped her eyes as she pulled away from her mentor's embrace. "At the naming ceremony they gave me a fancy dress and made me look like nobility, but I'm really a poor servant girl who brought great difficulty to her family. If you see me differently now I understand."

"I don't see you differently," Vanessa said. "In Aric's Army we are all equal. You are not a lower-class citizen here. I do not think you are worthless or useless because something happened to you that you can't control, and I don't think the others in the army will think that either. Of course, we must be careful these days as some have turned away from Aric due to the influence of the Shadow Walkers, but most people here are still good and trustworthy."

"Really?" *That sounds almost too good to be true. But I hope it is true.*

"Really," Vanessa replied. "In fact, I think you will find that a lot of people in Adhiren have similar stories. They have come from many different cities and villages, all with struggles of their own. I was rejected by over half my village, and my father was rejected by his wife. Here in Aric's Army we have found a community that supports us no matter what."

"Thank you for helping me," Arimay said. Her eyes grew wide for a moment. "You promise you won't tell anyone else? Not even one person?"

"I promise." Vanessa smiled. She blew out the lamp and they settled back under their covers.

"I hope one day my mother and sister will be able to come here too."

"I hope for that too. Maybe we could speak with Aric sometime and see if he has any ideas for how we could make that happen."

"I'd like that very much. Thank you, Vanessa."

Arimay had just closed her eyes when someone began frantically pounding on the door.

"Ah!" She sat up in bed wide eyed. The voice on the other side of the door was yelling as if they were in great pain.

"Vanessa!" the voice called. "Vanessa, I need your help!"

I know that voice, Arimay thought. Vanessa got up and ran to the door, opening it to find a very distressed-looking Brianna. Her beautiful blonde hair was a mess and her eyes were red and swollen. Arimay's heart sank. She had never seen Vanessa's cheery friend look so miserable.

"Brianna, what's wrong?" Arimay ran over to the door with her mentor and led Brianna inside.

"It's my mother," Brianna said. "She's been taken by the Shadow Walkers."

A sick feeling began to rise in Arimay's stomach. Vanessa went to check that the lock on the door was securely fastened. Hand on the hilt of her sword, Vanessa sat down in the middle of the room and gestured for Arimay and Brianna to do the same.

"She heard a strange noise in our front yard," Brianna blubbered, "she went outside to check. She said she'd only be a minute. I heard her talking to someone and thought it was one of the guards on night patrol. Then I heard a scream. We all rushed outside but it was too late. She was gone, and all that was left was a puff of smoke."

"Where are your sisters and your father?" Vanessa asked, putting a hand on Brianna's shoulder. "Are they okay?"

"They're with a few of the soldiers on patrol right now."

"They are welcome to come and take shelter with us," Vanessa said. She leaned forward to give her friend a hug. "I'm so sorry."

Arimay knew what it was like to be without her mother. Her heart broke for Vanessa's friend. She reached over and hugged Brianna as well.

"This has got to stop," Brianna said, wiping her eyes. "Aric needs to put an end to this. Too many people have been taken. I want my mother back!" Her sadness had turned to anger.

"I know," Vanessa said in a calm, reassuring voice. "I want people back too. Aric says he has a plan. I really hope he is going to tell us what it is soon. I can't take much more of this either."

I wish Aric would make sense of this for us, Arimay closed her eyes and tried to go back to sleep. *He will put his plan into action now. He has to. So many people are suffering.*

CHAPTER TEN

THE NEXT MORNING VANESSA, Arimay, Brianna and Alexander walked wearily together to the Emera Fields for the daily meeting. Vanessa was surprised to see only about one hundred people had gathered. She met up with Dillan while her friends visited with other soldiers they knew from Emeraldia. The two friends embraced as they shook off the chill of the miserable things that had happened in the night.

"Do you think many people were taken in the night?" she asked.

"I don't know." Dillan shrugged. "I saw one family on my street on the way here and asked if they were coming and they said no, they are too tired from fighting off the Shadow Walkers last night. A couple other soldiers said the presence of the Shadow Walkers is a fact of life that we have to deal with now. They didn't think Aric will ever come up with a plan to defeat them."

Vanessa stared at her friend in shock. As she listened to the conversations of other soldiers around her, a similar attitude was being expressed:

"Ten more missing, just another day in Adhiren."

"Our numbers are down by twenty percent today, business as usual."

"Aric has failed us. I don't know why we keep meeting like this when nothing is changing."

"I don't see the point of having that many soldiers on night guard anymore. People are going to leave no matter what we do."

"We should go back to how things were before all of this started."

Vanessa clenched her fists and let out an exasperated breath. "I can't believe this," she muttered.

Dillan tried to hold her back, but Vanessa shot him a glance that said, "Don't try to stop me." He took a step back with his hands raised in surrender as Vanessa went charging into a group of unsuspecting people.

"Hey!" she shouted. "Why are you talking like that?"

The conversations ceased and everyone turned to stare at her. One of the soldiers spoke up. "Talking like what, Vanessa?"

"Like the Shadow Walkers aren't a threat to our country anymore. Like hundreds of people haven't been led away by their lies into lives of suffering. Like you couldn't be one of the people who get taken away tonight if you're not careful."

An older soldier, about fifty years of age, patted Vanessa on the head as if she were a small child, which made her tense her shoulders and clench her fists even tighter.

"Settle down, young one," the older soldier chided, "you think you know so much, but you have not been here long. You are very naïve if you think Aric is going to be able to solve this one. If he could, he would have done so months ago. It would be best to focus on protecting the family you have left, and not get your hopes up for some grand rescue scheme. Save your energy."

"The Shadow Walkers are here for now," an older lady added in a monotone voice. "You have to accept that. We can't make them go away, and we need to get back to our regular duties. Worrying about them, and the people that are lost, does not make them go away. We cannot fight them off, so we need to stop trying and save our energy for other matters. If people are going to walk away, they are going to walk away. There's not much we can do about it."

"How can you believe that?" Vanessa asked, wide-eyed. "Haven't you lost friends and family members to the Shadow Walkers? Do you not care about them at all? My friend Jareth was taken by them and he is not okay. They are hurting him. They are sending him to kill people. Who knows what other terrible things he is being forced to do and he may not even realize it. My best friend just lost her *mother* last night. And I nearly lost my apprentice. This is not okay. Are you not concerned for your loved ones being taken and treated like this? Don't you want to fight to get them back?"

The soldier she was addressing looked at her and shrugged. "We cannot change the way things are, Vanessa." He patted her on the head once again. "You will upset people if you continue to act like this. Better to save yourself and accept the Shadow Walkers now than get angry about it."

"I don't think people are angry enough," Vanessa said.

"You had better get control of your young lady," the soldier turned to address Dillan, who had joined the group when he heard Vanessa's voice getting louder.

"My...my young lady?" Dillan stammered. Vanessa blushed.

"She's right, you know," Dillan cleared his throat and looked sternly at the soldier who had been speaking to her.

"You believe what you want, and I'll believe what I want," came the reply. "Ain't going to make a difference either way."

"Ugh!" Vanessa stomped off away from the crowd, unable to meet their gazes.

"Hey," Dillan called after her.

"Thanks for standing up for me," Vanessa said softly after she took a deep breath. Her fists still clenched. She turned around to face him.

"Any time," Dillan replied. "I agree with you, and I think many others do as well. Hopefully Aric will have some good news today."

"Vanessa," King Aric called. She turned around to see him standing right behind her.

"It isn't right." Vanessa sighed, tears beginning to flow.

"I know," Aric replied.

"How can they talk about their lost loved ones like that? Like they don't matter? How can they talk about *you* like that? It's not normal for Shadow Walkers to be in Adhiren and take people away. It isn't okay that they're hurting so many people. Why doesn't anyone care anymore?"

Aric put his hand on Vanessa's shoulder. "Your friends still care. And I care very much. My heart breaks for everyone who has been hurt by Malik and his servants. The soldiers who remain here may not have been led away in the middle of the night by the Shadow Walkers, but many are starting to believe their lies during the day. They have not taken proper precautions and as a result what is whispered to them in the dark is staying in their minds when they wake. Even now, there are many members of this army who doubt their loyalty to me and to Adhiren because of the Shadow Walkers. They will try to get others to see things the way they do. In the end, they will also be taken if they do not come to their senses."

"Are you going to set them straight? Tell them the truth? Are you going to save them?"

"If I tell them the truth right now, they will not believe me."

"Then what are you going to do? Can you make them believe you?"

"For the moment, I can do nothing. My father and I are working on a plan, but it is not yet complete. When it is, we will deal a significant blow to Malik and rescue the people he has taken from us once and for all."

"People are saying you keep using that as an excuse." Vanessa turned away from Aric's gaze and kicked the dirt with her foot. "That you really can't defeat the Shadow Walkers and don't want us to know that."

"And what do you believe, Vanessa?"

She hesitated a moment. "I...I've seen...I know...you can do this, right King Aric?" She looked up at her king, eyes beginning to water once again. "You can end this evil and bring back our loved ones? You won't let them suffer forever?"

"Yes, dear one, but the time is not yet right. Will you trust me?"

"Yes," Vanessa replied quietly. A weak smile spread across her face. "Please stop the Shadow Walkers soon. I can't take much more of this, and neither can my friends and family."

Aric embraced her. "You have fought well, Vanessa. I see great strength in you. Your loyalty and the loyalty of your friends means a lot to me in this troubled time. I wish I could tell you more right now, but when the plan is complete you will understand why I could not explain it sooner."

Her king's words did not make much sense, but she had learned her lesson years ago about trying to solve problems without his guidance. When she had ventured off the path he marked on the map for her in Tar'Máran she ended up being one of Malik's prisoners. *Whatever the plan is,* she thought, *it's going to work. It has to.*

"Vanessa!" Arimay called to her from where her friends were standing. She was waving her arms excitedly. The morning training session was about to begin. "Thank you, Aric."

* * *

It didn't take long for the Shadow Walkers to become even bolder. They were soon seen roaming the streets in broad daylight. Patrol duties never ceased and Vanessa found herself walking up and down her street more in a week than she had in the past two years. Since she was too young to fight on her own, Arimay accompanied Vanessa on her patrol shifts, partially to see what the responsibility included and partly so she wouldn't find herself sitting alone in Vanessa and Alexander's house. Brianna, her sisters and her father had also moved in with them since the loss of their mother. They figured there was strength in numbers and they needed all the strength and support they could get. Aiyanna and Jahzara spent most of their days playing inside the house while the adults took turns watching them. Aiyanna's nightmares had gotten worse, and Jahzara was starting to have them too. This made for a full time job for Vanessa, Brianna and Arimay as they chased away Shadow Walkers both inside and outside their home.

When they felt as if they couldn't survive any longer, the Doves would appear and sing a beautiful song unlike any they had heard anywhere else. As they sang, their strength would be renewed and they would find they could keep going after all, even for a little bit longer. As the days turned into weeks and months Vanessa, Alexander, Arimay and Brianna found there were fewer and fewer people they could trust. Many soldiers had accepted the existence of the Shadow Walkers and given up all hope of their lives changing for the better. Others began to respond aggressively to those who continued to use up all their strength to keep the Shadow Walkers away. They called them fools and disturbers of the peace. There were now enemies all around them, and only some of them could be chased away by the swords from Aric.

Aric remained mostly silent on the matter, although his face would often reveal that he too was exhausted and enraged at how his people were being treated. He continued to have important meetings with his father at the Emerald Palace but no one, not even the Doves, had revealed to the remaining faithful soldiers anything about these meetings or when a solution would be reached.

* * *

"And that," Vanessa said, "was how I learned where the Blackstone Village was, and how scary angry bears are!"

Arimay laughed as she finished braiding Vanessa's hair. "I can picture it now," she said. "Brave Hero Vanessa, lost in the woods, screaming like a little girl and trying to scare away a giant bear with a tiny stick."

A fluttering noise at the window distracted them from their conversation.

"A Dove!" Arimay gasped.

"Do you have a message for us?" Vanessa asked with a polite nod in the bird's direction.

"We have been sent throughout the land," the Dove began, "to deliver a most urgent message from King Aric himself."

Finally, Vanessa thought. *He's going to put his plan into action.*

"What's the message?" Arimay asked.

"He says the suffering of his people has gone on long enough and he plans to put a stop to it."

Vanessa let out a sigh of relief.

"Tomorrow morning, just after the sun rises, Aric will be holding a very important meeting. Malik is coming to the Emerald Palace to speak with him."

"Malik is coming *where*?"

"Do not fret, young ones. My Master has everything under control. For your safety he has ordered that no soldiers other than ones he has specifically assigned to guard duty for this task may enter the palace tomorrow under any circumstances. Malik has said he is not interested in harming you at the moment, but of course, we do not trust him to keep his word."

"How is Aric going to defeat him?" Arimay asked.

"That will be revealed in due time," the Dove responded. "After the meeting, Aric will give us instructions for what to do next. We will come to you and share whatever information we are given at that time. For now, stay close to home and keep up your regular duties in the fight against the Shadow Walkers."

"We will," Vanessa replied.

"I must be off," the Dove concluded. "Long live the king."

"Long live the king!" Vanessa and Arimay called after the Dove as it took to the sky.

Moments later Alexander burst through the door, looking as if he had been running for days. "Vanessa, Arimay, have you heard the news?"

"Yes," they both replied with a grim expression.

"Where are Brianna and the others?"

"They went for a walk," Arimay answered. "They'll be back soon."

"Good." Alexander sighed. "I don't want any of you to venture near the palace tomorrow, for any reason. Do you understand?"

"Yes."

"Okay. I'm heading out for another patrol shift. By the grace of Aric I hope we will be closer to victory tomorrow evening than we are now."

* * *

"Vanessa?" a small voice whispered in the dark of night.

"Yes?" Vanessa replied groggily.

"I want to go to the palace tomorrow morning."

Vanessa sat up to face her apprentice. "Arimay," she whispered, "you heard what my father said."

"I know, but don't you want to know what is going on? To maybe see some of it with your own eyes? Maybe Aric is going to fight Malik. Wouldn't you like to see that?"

"I would," Vanessa admitted. "But how can we do that?"

"We could hide in the crowd," Arimay suggested. "We could wear clothes that don't have any bright colours on them. We could pretend to be market workers or something. I'm really good at keeping my head down and not being noticed. I could show you how to do it."

"You know what, that's not such a bad idea." *She's pretty convincing when she makes up her mind to do something.*

"If you're going then I'm coming too," Brianna whispered, trying her best not to wake her little sisters who were sleeping beside her. "There's no way my best friend is getting to see this without me."

"Then it's settled," Vanessa said. "I guess we're going." She crept to her closet to find a few dresses in neutral colours. She tossed one to Arimay and one to Brianna. Quickly and quietly they got dressed and tip toed to the door. It made a creaking noise as they opened it. Arimay cringed. Vanessa turned around to see Alexander standing in the living room, arms folded across his chest.

"I had a feeling you wouldn't be able to resist," he sighed, shaking his head.

"We were thinking…" Vanessa began.

"I know what you were thinking," he replied. "The truth is I was thinking it too. If you must go, I will come with you."

"What about my sisters?" Brianna asked. She turned to her two sleeping siblings.

Brianna's father stirred. He sat up to face his eldest daughter. "Brianna," he said, "I have already lost your mother. Don't get yourself taken as well. My heart could not bear it. I wish you would stay here with me and your sisters."

"Father, I must go," Brianna whispered. "Vanessa, her father, and many other people will be looking out for me. We have our swords from Aric. We will be alright." She bent down to gently kiss her father's forehead. "I will come back. Please look after them."

"May Aric guide your journey. Do not stay away long, dear one."

"Alexander," Brianna's father warned. "Make sure no harm comes to my daughter. The honour of your family now depends on it."

"Of course." Alexander gave a solemn and respectful nod. "Let me get some food and we'll be on our way."

* * *

Loyal soldiers of Aric were full of rage the next morning as they stood outside Emeraldia's gates waiting for a glimpse of their unwelcome guest. They threw rotten fruit and jeered at the guards stationed there.

"How could you let this happen?" they cried. "Our city is doomed!" Vanessa and her friends weaved through the crowd, trying to get a better view of the proceedings. *I guess other people didn't follow the instructions either.*

Soldiers were stationed at the city gates and along the route to the palace to keep people away from Malik and his troops. The crowd began to shift as a group of dark soldiers came marching toward the palace in straight, rigid lines. A black and red caravan approached the gates consisting of horses, terrifying-looking animals and some of Malik's most recent human slaves.

"Ow!" Vanessa cried. Someone had bumped into her.

"Sorry," the familiar voice replied.

Vanessa turned around. "Dillan?"

"Yep."

"You're here too?"

"So is Gaerwin. He's around here somewhere. I didn't recognize you in that outfit, until you turned around and I saw your…"

"Beautiful brown eyes?" Vanessa held her hands up to her face, blinked, and smiled.

Dillan laughed and turned his gaze toward the ground. He shuffled his feet awkwardly. "I'd recognize your face in any crowd, Vanessa."

"I'm sorry I can't come to Emeraldia to visit you very often," she said. "There's been so much going on."

"That's okay," Dillan reassured her. "We've been quite busy here too. So are you in disguise or…?"

"Arimay said it would be a good idea to not draw attention to myself," Vanessa whispered. "Unfortunately I'm followed a lot of places I go now, and I didn't want to put anyone in danger because of that."

"Smart kid."

"Malik will be here any minute."

"I know." Dillan shuddered. They stood together to watch the dark soldiers approach. They grasped cach other's hands tightly as Malik's army got closer. A dark feeling of dread hung over the soldiers of Aric who had gathered. As if in response to the events happening below, dark clouds moved in over the palace and the gathered crowd.

Then they saw him. Malik was being carried in a palanquin by four emaciated human slaves. Their bodies bent under the weight of the palanquin. Sweat poured from their brows.

He was in his half-man, half-dragon form—the one he preferred to use when appearing in public. He waved to the crowd in mockery, as if he were an honoured dignitary from another realm who was gracing them with his presence. He was acting as if this was all some sort of sick joke.

The residents of Emeraldia booed, spat and raised their swords in protest as Malik entered their great city. They were under strict orders from Aric not to attack the dark army, but that didn't mean they could not express their disgust in other ways. Soon the repulsive caravan disappeared from view as it approached the entrance to the palace. The flustered crowd huddled together and waited to hear from the Doves.

* * *

Khalon stood rigid in his assigned place in the throne room. Aric's father, the High King of the world, was standing next to him on his right, and Aric was on his left. He tried his best to suppress his anger but his face would not allow him to hide his true feelings about Aric's plan. His hands gripped his sword tightly, ready to strike the moment Malik tried to attack the king or himself. He was certain it would happen. Today he would end Malik's reign once and for all.

The double doors to the throne room swung open and the hideous dragon-man pranced in, accompanied by two billowing Shadow Walkers bearing sinister smiles.

"Aric!" he exclaimed, swooping down into an irreverent bow. "It's been too long. How are things?"

"You know exactly why you were called here today," Aric replied firmly.

"Oh, you're not upset about my new recruitment methods, are you? What are a few hundred measly humans to you anyway?"

"Those people are under my protection."

"Fine job you're doing of protecting them right now."

"Hurting even one of my people is a serious matter, Malik."

"What are you going to do about it? They don't even want to come back to you anymore."

"You have hurt my people, and I won't let you get away with it any longer."

"*Your* people? Oh you naïve little king. This is *my* world, Aric. It has been mine since you kicked me out of your army. Did you honestly expect not to suffer the consequences for that? I am now the best and most powerful ruler in the entire world, like I was always meant to be. And I will punish you for what you did to me. I will take away everything you love, all of your people and your country. They are mine. There is nothing you can do, my power is far too great. And once I have them all in my possession, I'll be coming back for you. I'm going to end this once and for all!"

With a grim facial expression, Aric met the eyes of his adversary. "I want to propose a deal with you, Malik. My father and I have discussed it thoroughly." He turned to face the High King and nodded, signaling his turn to speak.

"The deal is this," the High King's deep voice rang out. "You will stop hurting the people of my son's army. If they want to return here instead of fighting for you, you will let them. In exchange we will give you something far greater."

Malik twiddled his long, clawed fingers with delight. "What could you possibly give me that I don't already have, old man?"

Aric rose from his throne. "Me."

Gasps of shock came from the soldiers present.

"What did you say?"

"You will take me as your slave, and let the others go free."

Malik cackled. "You want to rescue them? After all they've done to you? They don't love you anymore, Aric. They don't want to serve you, they want you dead! They don't want to be freed."

"I wouldn't expect you to understand, but these people are very dear to me. I promised to protect and help them, and that's what I'm going to do, whatever the cost."

"Whatever the cost," Malik said. "It's your funeral."

He signaled to his sinister companions, who both produced flaming whips at their fingertips. One flung theirs out and wrapped it around Aric's left ankle, pulling him to the ground face-first. The other bound Aric's hands and feet with similar flaming ropes. Malik created his own flaming whip and began to lash the king's back, leaving painful, burning wounds. Aric cried out in pain.

Khalon lunged forward and swung his sword at Malik. He had never heard Aric make that sound before. "That's enough! You're not taking him." His blade sliced off one of Malik's ears.

"Khalon," Aric gasped, looking up at the commander. "No. This is not how I want you to fight." The king closed his eyes, stretched out one hand as far as he could move it, and a golden light began to shine around him. The light traveled up to Malik's head and restored his ear where Khalon had sliced it off.

Malik touched his newly restored ear with his clawed hand and let out a gleeful laugh. "Nice try," he hissed, then held an outstretched hand to Khalon. Red light coursed through his hand and shot out from it toward the commander. Khalon fell over and groaned in pain as his own ear was severed and a long cut was left on his face. "That'll teach you not to be heroic."

"You have to let him take me," Aric spoke. Khalon looked up to face his king. His amber eyes were not full of light as they usually were. "Trust me, Khalon."

"Yes, nothing you can do about it," Malik cackled. "Now let's get a move on, shall we?" He snapped his fingers and the Shadow Walkers surrounded them in a cloud of smoke. In a moment they, along with Aric and Malik had disappeared. The entire throne room was engulfed in shocked silence.

* * *

Khalon winced as the High King held bandages full of stinging medicine against his wounds. Tears began to roll down his face as he thought of Aric, who was now being tortured at the hands of the most vile being he had ever had the misfortune to know.

"You," Khalon gasped, turning to face the High King. "You let Malik do this. Why did you let him do this? Why didn't you stop him?"

"It was not my place."

"Not your place? Aric is your *son*! Do you not care about him? Do you not care about us, his army, who are now without their leader?"

"I do."

"Then what in the world is going on here?"

The High King placed a hand on Khalon's shoulder. He felt a sense of calm begin to course through his body and he lowered his sword as Aric's father spoke. "This is part of our plan, Khalon. Aric and I came up with it together. I know it doesn't make much sense right now, but we are actually leading Malik into a trap. By becoming his slave, Aric is placing himself at the heart of Malik's operations. In a few days' time, he and I are going to combine our power and deal a blow to Malik that he will never recover from."

"So what is our part in all of this?"

"I need you and my son's army to wait here," the High King explained. "I will be sending you and Tarak instructions through the Doves. We will defeat the Army of Darkness and set all of our people free."

It sounded too good to be true. *Malik defeated, once and for all? But if anyone could do it, it would be Aric and his father.*

"Of course, Your Majesty." Khalon bowed to the High King in submission. When he raised his head, Aric's father was gone and he was left with the three other trembling soldiers.

"Come on," he urged them, heading for the door. "Someone has to tell the rest of the army what happened."

* * *

Khalon and Tarak sent Doves to summon the remaining loyal members of Aric's Army to the entrance of the Emerald Palace. When they arrived, he explained the events that had taken place in the throne room. Before he could get to the High King's instructions, the people began to draw their own conclusions.

"Aric has abandoned us!" one woman cried.

"There's no way he can escape from Malik now," another added.

"We're all going to die!"

Khalon let out a sigh and wiped his brow. "Aric's father has promised that this is all part of their plan," he said, trying very hard to believe the words himself.

"We will be hearing more of it from the Doves in the coming days. Aric seemed adamant that even one soldier being enslaved by Malik is too many and that he was going to fix it. I don't fully understand it, but for now we have to trust that he and the High King know what they're doing. They have dealt with Malik much longer than we have, after all."

Discontented murmurs arose from the crowd.

"The High King has ordered us to wait for news from the Doves, after which we will help with Aric's mission to destroy Malik once and for all."

More discontented murmurs arose from the crowd.

"That's a terrible idea," one man retorted. "You must have misunderstood what the High King was telling you. Surely he does not want us to sit here and do nothing!"

"If you want to leave, then leave," Khalon said. "If you no longer trust Aric and his father to help us defeat Malik, you do not have to stay. But I am going to stay here and follow his instructions. Aric has done so much for us, it is only right that we stand with him now."

Much to Khalon's disappointment, many people turned and walked away at his invitation. They grumbled to themselves about the foolishness of ever trusting King Aric to save them and all the time and effort they had wasted as they looked back with contempt at the twelve people that remained.

There was a man standing in the middle of the group that Khalon recognized. He was Alexander Handeraz, the man whose daughter Vanessa had led people from

Leftrock Village to Adhiren to escape the wrath of Malik. She was there too, as were nine others. Some were young like Vanessa, and there was one older, frail-looking woman. A dark-haired girl no older than ten stood with the group, shaking as she willed herself not to run away. They hardly looked like an army fit to defeat the Dark King.

If this is the will of Aric and his father, then so be it.

"Thank you for your loyalty," Khalon spoke as his voice trembled.

As he spoke a Dove fluttered down to meet the group and landed on Khalon's shoulder.

"I bring news from Aric's father," it chirped.

"What is the High King's will?" Tarak asked the bird.

"The High King says this: Stay together. Support one another. Only by doing this shall we defeat the Army of Darkness."

"He wants us to march on Hadriar," Khalon speculated.

"That's not quite what the Dove said." Alexander spoke up.

"Does anyone have another suggestion?" Khalon asked.

The group fell silent. No one knew what they could possibly do to help end Malik's reign of terror. When no other interpretations were offered, Khalon cleared his throat. "We cannot continue to stay here and hide in our homes as we have been doing for so long. It has not helped the people who have been taken. We must act, and we will act together. We are going to march on Hadriar. We will be leaving at sundown.

Each of you must bring a horse, your best weapons, and provisions."

As the group of twelve dispersed to make their preparations, Khalon turned to Tarak. The commander had been standing beside him during the entire speech but had said nothing.

"It doesn't look good, does it?" Khalon asked.

"No," Tarak replied shaking his head, "it sure doesn't. By all logic it would seem this plan is doomed to fail."

"What other choice do we have? We can't just walk away."

"No. We can't."

CHAPTER ELEVEN

THE SOMBER GROUP LED their horses out the gates of Emeraldia at sundown that evening. Khalon and Tarak led the way, and Alexander and Jason brought up the rear. Between them were the rest of Aric's remaining faithful followers: Vanessa, Brianna, Arimay, Dillan, Gaerwin, Nimeesha, Helena, and Jason's wife Lillian. Vanessa's adoptive father, Menawa, had also joined the group, leaving his wife at home to protect her brother Caleb should any Shadow Walkers enter their home. They didn't look like a powerful army about to take down the most powerful villain in the world, but that's what they were attempting to do.

"A small chance is better than no chance," Gaerwin commented when Dillan had calculated their odds of survival.

The group rode their horses through the night to the beautiful hedged city of Gal'Mesh.

"We will rest here," Khalon explained. "We as well as the horses need all of our strength for the battle ahead, and there may be still some in this city who are loyal to Aric and his cause. It will be best for us to approach Hadriar under the cover of darkness. We will enter Tar'Máran tomorrow evening."

Even after hundreds of Gal'Meshans had joined Aric's Army at the Battle of the Emera Fields, many people who lived there chose not to side with Aric or Malik. Vanessa was unsure of how much support they would find there.

They rode to the centre of the city where Khalon and Tarak greeted Lennea, the Guardian of the city. Her eyes were much brighter and full of life than they were when she and Vanessa had crossed paths two years before.

"Welcome to Gal'Mesh," Lennea greeted them with her soft voice. "How may we assist you, servants of King Aric?"

"It is wonderful to see you again," Tarak replied with a slight bow. "My friends and I require shelter and rest. We are on our way to fight Malik, to get back our king and the rest of our people."

"You embark on a perilous journey," Lennea observed. "You are free to use our guest housing but I cannot allow you to seek additional support here. The Shadow Walkers have infiltrated this city as well and have taken and killed many. As a result the people are no longer favourably disposed to your king." Her eyes began to well up with tears. "Your intentions are noble, and I sincerely hope you succeed." She turned and walked away from Tarak, covering her face with one hand.

"This way," Tarak said. He guided the weary soldiers and their horses to a place they could rest.

Vanessa crawled beneath the fresh white sheets in one of the guest rooms and quickly drifted off to sleep. She was not worried about bad dreams today. Her impending reality was much more frightening than anything the Shadow Walkers could come up with.

After a deep sleep that seemed to last only minutes, Arimay burst into Vanessa's room. "It's time!" she called cheerfully.

"Someone had a good rest," Vanessa moaned as she sat up. She covered her eyes for a moment until she adjusted to the warm yellow and orange hues the setting sun was casting over the city.

"Tarak says we leave in five minutes." Arimay turned and walked away, calling to Danilo as she headed to the stable.

The group walked beside their horses, holding on to their leads as they led them to the gates of Gal'Mesh. Dillan gently pushed past Brianna to walk beside Vanessa, his horse at his other side. Brianna was busy talking to her horse and didn't seem to mind.

"Looks pretty grim doesn't it," he said.

"Yeah." Vanessa sighed.

"We may not come out of this alive."

"Maybe not, but I'm trying not to think about that right now." Vanessa choked back tears as she turned away from Dillan's gaze to stare at the sunset.

"I can't stop thinking about it." Dillan sighed and drew in a deep breath. He stopped walking and turned to face Vanessa. "There are so many things I want to do. I want to have the chance to grow old, to start my own business, to train more soldiers for Aric's

Army..."

"I...I feel the same way," Vanessa said. "I'm not ready to die. But if this is Aric's will..."

Dillan reached out and held Vanessa's hand. "Whatever happens," he said, "we will go through it together."

"Friends of Adhiren," Khalon said, interrupting their conversation. "Those who have remained loyal to our king even to this end, from here on we are riding into battle. May the Doves help us in this dreaded hour. Long live the king!"

"Long live the king!" the group replied. Then they mounted their horses to follow Khalon out the gates of Gal'Mesh and toward the entrance to Tar'Máran.

Aside from a few whispered comments between Vanessa, Dillan and Brianna, the group grew increasingly quiet and unsettled as they neared the entrance to Tar'Máran. They were heading straight to the heart of Malik's kingdom and were unsure what unpleasant things they would find when they arrived there.

The city of Hadriar was silent as Aric's loyal soldiers approached its gates later that night. Not a single guard was on duty, and not a single torch was lit.

"Maybe they're all busy somewhere else?" Arimay whispered, fully knowing how ridiculous her reasoning sounded.

Khalon motioned for her to be silent. "Don't let down your guard," he warned. "Taking down Malik is not going to be easy."

Everyone dismounted their horses and led them

through the gates seemingly undetected. Dark buildings rose in every direction, indicating a city that was full of Malik's minions, and yet no one was out in the street. No movement could be seen through the windows.

It was too quiet, and too still. As if all the dark creatures in the land were holding their breath, waiting to pounce. Vanessa pulled out her sword and the light it emitted nearly blinded her. The others did the same. It was a reminder to them to never let down their guard, and the light was reassuring in a small way. A solitary Dove circled overhead, cooing once loudly before disappearing behind the dark clouds.

"That's the sign," Khalon said. "We're in the right place."

"I'm scared," Arimay whispered.

"So am I," Vanessa replied.

The group continued to walk through the city in silence. They could feel the grief and misery of the thousands of prisoners from Adhiren that had been captured and tortured at Malik's hand. They were sure some of them were in prison cells nearby, wishing they could end their suffering.

I hope we can end it today, Vanessa thought.

A shrill whistle cut through the gloom and sent shivers down Vanessa's spine. Before she could blink, dark miserable creatures crawled out of every crevice accompanied by the human slaves and their Shadow Walker masters, weapons in hand. The group dismounted and released their horses as they gathered in a circle, swords pointed to face their foes. Khalon let out a feeble battle cry and everything became a blur. Vanessa spun around to face snarling teeth, sharp claws, and the bruised and bloodied bodies of those who had used to fight alongside her. The Shadow Walkers hung back from the chaos, grinning with an eerie sort of pleasure as they controlled their victims. It grieved her to injure former soldiers, but she knew they would kill her and her friends without hesitation if given the opportunity.

A feeble cry tore through Vanessa's senses and stopped her momentarily in her tracks. Helena had fallen. A Dark soldier had driven a spear through her chest, causing her to collapse. Her sword had been knocked away beyond her reach. There were so many creatures between her and where Vanessa stood that she couldn't do anything except watch it happen in slow motion. *Just like my nightmare,* she recalled. She saw a Shadow Walker smirk at her realization.

"Helena!" she called.

Her dear old friend gave her a contented smile and closed her eyes as her body stopped trembling. "I'll be fine, Vani," she sighed as she took her last breath.

"No!" Vanessa screamed. She channeled her anger and grief into stabbing every vile creature that crossed her path with a ferocity she had never felt before.

It wasn't long before she heard another familiar voice. A frightened scream that could only have come from her apprentice cut through the chaos. Arimay had fallen, with a stab wound in her arm and a long bloody cut across her face. She trembled as her hand reached for a piece of her sword that had been trampled by Malik's soldiers. She looked so helpless and afraid, like a baby lamb being led to the slaughter. Vanessa remembered Naara, and what she must have looked like as the terrible fire closed in on her village. What the realization on her face must have looked like when she realized she wouldn't survive. *I can't save Naara, or Helena, but I will not lose another friend. Not today.*

"Run!" Vanessa yelled as she dodged another blow. "Arimay, run, and don't look back! Find somewhere safe to hide. We'll come back for you later."

With a quick nod the girl ducked and crawled as fast as she could away from the danger. She was gone from Vanessa's sight within seconds as Bogdan, Malik's right-hand rhino-man, made his appearance.

"Nice to see you again," he hissed through his rotting teeth. Vanessa raised her sword to attack him, but lost her balance and ended up being the recipient of a blow to the head from the butt of his staff. She growled as she wiped the blood from her face. She dropped her sword and turned to face him, fists raised. *That's it, you're going down.*

She raised her arm to punch him, but something restricted her movement. Someone had a tight grip on her arm. She writhed to try and get away but it was no use. Then she heard an all-too familiar sound. *Clink.* Handcuffs.

She could feel hot breath on her shoulder, and when she turned and saw the clawed hand holding her captive fresh anger surged through her veins.

"Malik," she spat. "Let me go. You know you won't win this."

"Why hello Dearie," the evil king replied in a sickeningly sweet voice. "So nice of you to drop by. I'd grown quite fond of you when you were my prisoner here before. I think if you take a look around you will see that I am, in fact, winning."

The fighting had ceased and Vanessa and her friends were all in handcuffs, restrained by Malik's foul creatures and guarded by the Shadow Walkers. Khalon wore a look of deep sadness on his face that Vanessa had never seen before. Tarak wouldn't even lift his gaze from the ground. Her father was kneeling, head bowed, too weak to stand. But Arimay wasn't there. *Thank goodness. Doves, please keep her safe.*

"I've got some wonderful accommodations set up for you," Malik cackled, "our finest prison cells have been prepared specifically for your 'surprise' visit. Here you will be treated to the full prison experience including starvation, torture, and ultimately death. I hope you enjoy your stay." He pushed Vanessa to the ground and turned to walk away.

"Oh, and one more thing," Malik turned around with a malicious grin on his face. "Jareth says hello."

That's it! Vanessa stood and prepared to charge after the foul king, forgetting that she lacked the use of her arms. Within seconds she fell face-first on the cold, hard ground and everything went black.

CHAPTER TWELVE

WHEN VANESSA OPENED HER EYES, she gasped and closed them immediately. She had seen the black iron bars and cold, concrete walls of Malik's prison. She heard the steady drip of water from a leaky pipe nearby, and the click-clack of black boots marching back and forth in the hallway. She tried to focus on her own breathing but it wasn't any use. She couldn't calm down. She had been there once before and was only saved by the arrival of the Doves. She didn't hear any of them now. *What's going to happen to me?*

Mustering up her courage, she opened her eyes again. She saw that she was in a tiny cell, and that more of the same cells surrounded her, spread out in a circle. There were small rectangular slats cut in the walls for air and light, so small that nothing could slip through them. She concluded that she was in one of the towers of Malik's Palace.

The other cells were occupied as well, with the others she had marched on Hadriar with as well as some other soldiers she didn't recognize. She spotted Alexander across the room, slumped over on the floor. *Is he breathing?*

"Father!" she cried. Her voice echoed through the room. "Father, wake up!"

"Now now, Missy," a dark soldier said as he approached her cell and unlocked the door. "We can't have anybody making a fuss. It makes our Master so terribly upset. Gives him an awful headache."

"Leave my father alone."

"Can't do that, sweetie. If you have a problem you'll have to take it up with the Boss himself." He whacked Vanessa in the head with the blunt end of his spear and she plunged back into darkness.

When she became conscious again, Vanessa heard someone crying. She opened her eyes to see Brianna huddled up in the cell next to hers. Her once-beautiful dress was all dirty, tattered and torn. Her long blonde hair had knots in it that would take weeks to remove. A Shadow Walker was lurking outside her cell with its arms folded across its chest.

"I miss her," Brianna cried. "I miss her so much."

"Then let me take you to her," the Shadow Walker hissed.

"I'd do anything to see her again." Her dark blue eyes welled with tears as she looked at the creature. It stepped forward and walked through the bars of her cell. It bent down as if to reassure her, and put a hand on her back.

"Brianna!" Vanessa crawled over as close as she could get to her friend. "Don't go. It's lying. They will hurt you!"

"You don't understand." Brianna's glare pierced Vanessa's heart and made her feel cold inside. "Your mother hasn't been taken. Your father is here with you. How could you possibly understand the choice I need to make right now."

"You're not thinking clearly," Vanessa pleaded. "Please don't go. I can't afford to lose another friend."

"You're not much of a friend if you want to keep me away from my family."

"Brianna."

"I have made my decision."

"Good," the creature hissed. It turned to Vanessa with a terrifying grin. "Your friend here has a lot to learn." It struck Vanessa on the face with its fiery whip. The cut stung terribly and blood began trickling down her neck. She cried out in pain and then fainted.

* * *

Vanessa awoke to Bogdan flashing her an eerie smile. She was out of her cell. He was sharpening a knife and licking his lips as he stared at her. She tried to sit up and spit in his face, but found that she could not move forward. Looking down she saw that she was strapped into a chair, held in place by restraints on her arms, chest and legs.

"Good morning," Bogdan said. "I'm so glad you're here. You and I are going to have a little chat."

"I would rather not."

"Unfortunately for you, Dearie," Bogdan replied, "you have no choice in the matter." He flashed his knife in front of her face and then held it firmly against her right arm. Vanessa winced.

"You are one of Aric's loyal soldiers, yes? I can only assume if he has some sort of hidden plan to overthrow my king he would have told you all about it."

"I don't know anything," Vanessa insisted.

"I don't believe you," Bogdan hissed. He pressed his face right up to hers. His foul breath made Vanessa want to gag.

"If you don't tell me what your king is planning, I shall cut you until you bleed to death. Is that understood?"

Vanessa glared at the dark soldier and did not say a word.

"Ah!"

Bogdan made the first cut.

"Ready to talk now?"

"I told you I don't know anything." Vanessa bit her lip and did her best to repress her tears.

"Liar." Bogdan made another slit on her arm. It stung like fire was coursing through her veins.

"Aric never told us what he was planning."

Another cut, this time on her left arm.

"All he said was to stay together and take care of each other!"

Another cut.

"Tell me what you *really* know," he said.

"That *is* what I really know."

Another cut.

Bogdan sighed in frustration and dropped the knife. "Clearly this isn't working. On to Phase Two."

What's Phase Two?

In a moment Bogdan returned with a flaming hot branding device on the end of a staff. The glowing hot metal was in the shape of a black bird.

"If you do not tell me what Aric is planning this instant, I will place this on your hand, over your precious Crest of Aric. Not only will you be in unfathomable pain, but your last remaining sign of your allegiance will be ruined forever."

Vanessa gave an exasperated sigh and closed her eyes. "I. Don't. Know. Anything."

Bogdan pressed the metal onto Vanessa's skin. She screamed and tried to pull away. Overwhelmed by the pain she felt her head tilting back and the sights and sounds around her beginning to fade. The last thing she heard before she lost consciousness was Bogdan speaking to another dark soldier. "This one is useless," he said. "Put her back with the others."

When the darkness had faded, Vanessa became acutely aware of her stomach growling. *Food,* she thought. *I haven't eaten in days.* She was back in her cell. She looked around the room and noticed that everyone else imprisoned there looked as thin and famished as she was. She turned to examine her wounds. The burn on her hand had blistered. She touched it lightly with her finger and immediately pulled it back. *It was still hot.* Just then, Bogdan walked down the corridor, tossing a juicy red apple up and down with his hand and whistling to himself.

Vanessa's mouth watered, and her stomach growled even louder as he came closer. Bogdan paused, looked around, and then met her gaze. "Was that you?" he asked.

Vanessa nodded.

"Are you hungry?"

Another nod.

"Would you like this sweet, juicy apple?" He held it in front of her, as close as he could get with the iron bars that were separating them.

"Please," she begged.

"Do you have any information you would like to share with me about your king?"

Vanessa shook her head vigorously. "I told you all that I know."

"Some help that was."

"Please, we're all starving."

"No useful information for me? No food."

Bogdan bit into the apple and juice from it sprayed Vanessa in the face. His loud crunching echoed through the room. He chewed with his mouth open for added dramatic effect. Soldiers moaned in agony and reached desperately toward the fruit. In response Bogdan laughed, then turned and walked away.

* * *

Later that day, a new prisoner was brought into the room. Bogdan roughly shoved a girl in a tattered, pale blue dress into the cell where Brianna had been and slammed the door shut. The girl fell forward on her face and cried out. *I know that voice*, Vanessa thought. *Where have I heard it before?*

She had long, straight, black hair with a dried-up

flower pinned to one side. Her skin was a few shades darker than Vanessa's, although exactly how dark was hard to tell in the dim lighting. She turned to take in her surroundings, and when she met Vanessa's gaze her eyes widened.

"My friend!" she gasped in a raspy voice, clinging to the metal bars. "Is it really you? Vanessa, from Leftrock Village?"

Vanessa's heart skipped a beat. The poor girl had a cut on her face and looked as if she hadn't bathed in weeks. But those eyes were unmistakable. "Naara?" She crawled forward to touch the girls' hand.

"Yes!" Naara replied, tears streaming down her face. "Yes, it's me! I asked Aric to let me see you again, and he did!"

"But how?"

"In the fire," Naara explained, "We did not get out before it started. But I did warn my parents. And then we saw one of the white birds."

"A Dove?"

"Yes, a Dove. We could not hear anything, and could not breathe very well, but we crawled through the forest following the Dove. We arrived in a safe place away from the fires and hid in a cave until it was over."

"And your parents…?"

"They are here too."

"I'm so sorry. I should have tried harder. I should never have left your village until you and your family came with me."

"Do not be sorry for me," Naara said. "It was not your fault. King Aric has welcomed me as a member of his

Army. I know he sent the Doves to help us. And I am glad that we get to see each other one last time."

The two friends held hands through the bars of their cells and cried, releasing their grief from what they had endured and their joy in seeing each other again.

"Have you really seen the Kingdom of the Sky?" Naara sniffled. "Back when you returned to my village, you said…"

"Yes," Vanessa used her arm to wipe her tears. "It's a beautiful place. We will be there soon."

"Until then, we will stay strong together."

Both girls did their best to lie down, attempting to get some rest. They kept one hand stretched out toward the other, with a few fingers touching through the bars.

It was a difficult task, sleeping on a cold, hard floor when she was starving, in intense pain, and bleeding from both arms, but Vanessa eventually succeeded. Over the next couple of days she was never really sure if she was dreaming or awake. Cries and screams surrounded her constantly, as did the click-clacking of the dark soldiers' boots as they kept an eye on their prisoners. She and Naara spoke to each other whenever they had enough strength to do so. Otherwise they sat in silence.

She worried about Brianna, Dillan, Arimay, her father and the others. *There's nothing I can do to help them. Aric, if you are ever going to act on that plan of yours it has to be now!*

* * *

After she had spent what felt like several years in the dark, miserable prison, Vanessa heard something that made her skin crawl even more than the bugs that slithered between the cells. It was the voice of Malik. And he sounded *happy*!

"Alright, everybody outside, chop chop! We don't have all day." Malik's slaves unlocked every cell in a zombielike fashion, leading the soldiers of Aric down a winding flight of stairs. They pushed and prodded the prisoners with staffs and sharp, pointy weapons, urging them to move faster.

Soon the entire prison had been assembled at the entrance to Malik's palace, save for King Aric. Malik was pacing back and forth in front of his literally captive audience as if he were anxiously awaiting something that no one else knew about. Vanessa spotted Arimay, Dillan and Alexander, but they were too far away to call out to them. She wasn't sure she even had enough strength to call to them if she got the chance. She desperately wanted to sit or lie down and rest, but she was securely held in place by cruel metal restraints.

"What's going on?" one soldier cried out.

"I am *so* glad you asked," Malik replied as he drummed his long, clawed fingers together. "I have gathered you all here today to show you once and for all that I am the most powerful being in the world. Today, I am going to kill your king."

Gasps of shock rose from the crowd. Vanessa and a few others lunged forward, wanting to attack Malik but held back by their restraints. She was immediately met with resistance and grunted in pain from the cold metal that was secured tightly against her chest.

"You can't do this!" another soldier cried. "You can't kill Aric!"

"Oh yes, yes I can," Malik replied. "Bogdan, bring him here!" Malik snapped his fingers to summon his assistant.

A moment later, Bogdan returned dragging a severely bloodied King Aric that hardly any of his soldiers recognized. He was so weak that he lay on the ground, not even able to raise his head. He had been severely tortured at the hand of Malik.

No, Vanessa thought, *not like this.*

"This is your king!" Malik cackled, "or at least, what used to be your king. I'm afraid he won't be able to defend himself very well now, will he?" Malik laughed some more as he pranced around Aric, nimbly stepping over him in some sort of macabre dance.

"This is your last chance, pathetic soldiers." Malik pointed his flaming spear at his captives. "Change your allegiance and join me before I kill your king, or I shall kill you the moment I am finished with him!"

Gasps and cries rose from the crowd.

"We will never join you," Alexander spat. The rest of the loyal soldiers murmured in agreement.

Malik shrugged, unhurt by their response. "Alright then." Bogdan handed him his sharpest spear. "One last chance, Aric." He pointed the spear squarely at

Aric's chest. "Join me and live as a slave in the most powerful army in the world, or die a painful death."

A solitary Dove flew to King Aric and he whispered something in its ear. The bird flew up into the sky, toward a single ray of light that was bursting through the clouds. Aric coughed and sputtered as he replied, "I will never join you, Malik."

"I knew you'd say that." The Dark King raised his arm to kill Aric. The crowd gasped. Some began to cry and others turned away from the scene. Just as Malik was about to strike, the ground shook, causing him to lose his balance.

"Argh!" Malik exclaimed as he fell and lost his grip on his spear. Unimpressed, he dusted himself off, stood up and reached for the spear again.

A loud voice boomed from the sky. "It is time."

Malik shuddered at the voice. Many of the soldiers trembled in fear.

Vanessa smiled. She knew who it was: the High King of the World! A bright beam of light shot out of the sky and landed on Aric's chest. He took a deep breath, and suddenly his face was glowing and light was shooting out from his hands and feet. He rose from the ground and his metal bindings snapped. In mere moments he had been transformed so that it no longer looked like he had ever spent even a moment in Malik's prison.

"Stand back," Aric ordered the crowd with a smile on his face. "Move away from the palace so I can deal with this foul creature once and for all."

The ugly creatures holding Aric's soldiers back obeyed, and the entire audience around the battlefield stepped away from the dark stone building.

Malik snorted and took a cautious step away from Aric, unsure of what to make of this new development.

"Your fight is not with them," Aric addressed his adversary, "it is with me."

With a growl, Malik lunged at Aric but the King of Adhiren swatted him away like he would a fly. Another rumble shook the earth, this time causing a large crack between the entrance of the palace and the place where the soldiers of both armies stood. Aric and Malik wrestled with each other as pieces of the palace walls began to crumble around them. Vanessa gasped when she realized what was happening. The palace was falling apart beneath the two fighting kings, and would soon plummet into the pit of lava that lay beneath it! *That's why Aric told us to move away,* she realized. *This must have been part of his plan!* The soldiers of both armies continued to look on, wide-eyed and open-mouthed, from their side of the ground that wasn't collapsing into the pit.

Vanessa had never seen such viciousness in Aric's eyes as he grappled with his enemy. Malik was bloodied and bruised, but Aric was not without his wounds. Malik proved to be a very formidable enemy. She really wasn't sure which of them was going to win, although she hoped with all of her heart it would be Aric.

Another loud crack echoed through the battlefield. Lightning struck the ground Aric and Malik were standing on and fire began to spew out of it. The ground shook and began to plummet toward the lava.

No! There was nothing she could do to help Aric now.

The small army stared at this turn of events with wide eyes. They were completely helpless. *Please Aric,* Vanessa pleaded, *please don't die.*

A swarm of Doves broke through the clouds and flew toward their king as he plummeted toward the pit. There was a bright flash of light and a splash of lava as the palace came crashing down on top of the two kings. The birds scattered and flew high into the sky and were seen no more. Vanessa shielded her eyes from the light.

The Shadow Walkers vanished in a puff of smoke, and Malik's enslaved army fell to the ground with a thud in one sudden movement. Then there was nothing but silence. Neither Aric nor Malik emerged from the pit. The entire world held its breath.

CHAPTER THIRTEEN

VANESSA LOOKED AROUND the desolate battlefield. There was no one left to fight, and no one left to protect them either. *What's going to happen to us?*

A loud clanging noise cut through the dismal atmosphere. The metal bonds on her wrists, ankles, and around her chest suddenly snapped open. She swayed as she tried to steady herself. The rest of Aric's Army had been freed as well. They gasped in shock as their chains fell to the ground and they collapsed from exhaustion.

From where she lay on the ground, she saw a few people moving, but most were still. Arimay and Jareth were lying on the ground nearby. *Are they dead?* She willed herself to stand, putting all her weight on her arms as she tried to push herself up.

A low rumble echoed throughout the decimated courtyard. It became louder and louder until it shook the entire battlefield. Vanessa panicked and held her arms out to steady herself. *Maybe it's the volcano. It's going to erupt!*

A mighty earthquake shook Tar'Máran until Vanessa and everyone else who had managed to stand up had fallen over again. A couple people hit their heads so hard on the ground that they lost consciousness. Everything fell silent.

After a few moments people began to stir. Vanessa held her head and groaned in agony as she tried to stand up. She noticed the others were struggling to stand as well. They were complaining about their aches and pains, but also visibly grateful to be alive.

"Where are we?" they asked. "What happened?"

As her vision came back into focus Vanessa saw Jareth sitting nearby, examining his bruised and bloodied arms as if they were not his own. He turned and met her gaze. The dead look had left his eyes and they were once again full of light and life, as they had been what felt like so long ago.

"Jareth?" Vanessa asked, trembling as she cautiously crawled toward her old friend. She realized she did not have a weapon to defend herself if he tried to hurt her again. She sat down close to him, but far enough away that she could retreat if necessary.

"It's me, Vanessa." she spoke gently. "Do you remember me?"

Jareth's eyes widened and he immediately turned away from her gaze. "Please don't hurt me," he said, raising his arms feebly in front of his face.

"I'm not going to hurt you." She was a little surprised by his response.

"But I deserve it," Jareth said, shaking. "I...I tried to kill you." Tears began to roll down his cheeks. "The

Shadow Walkers were controlling me. I didn't know what I was doing."

"I know."

"I don't really want to kill you, Vanessa."

"I know." Vanessa pulled her injured friend into an embrace. "The Shadow Walkers are gone now. They can't hurt you anymore."

"Vanessa!" Arimay hobbled over and embraced her mentor. "I'm so glad you're alive."

"I'm glad you're alive too," Vanessa replied. "I was so worried when I lost sight of you when we first arrived here."

"What happened?"

"I don't know," Vanessa said. "I don't think anybody knows."

"Ben!" an enthusiastic voice called. The trio turned to see Jason, the man Vanessa and Arimay had helped save from the Shadow Walkers in Kalmehara. He was running with open arms toward a blonde-haired boy who looked no older than ten. The boy laughed and then started to cry as he embraced his father. His mother Lillian ran over to embrace him as well.

"I thought Ben was dead," Arimay said. "Devoured by the Shadow Walkers when they first came to Adhiren."

"That's what the creature said. How can this be?"

"Vani!" A familiar voice rang out through the crowd. Vanessa turned to see her old friend walking toward her.

"Helena!" Vanessa stood up and rushed over to greet her oldest friend. "You're alive! But how? You got hurt.

I saw you die."

"It was the strangest thing." Helena laughed. "One moment I was lying on the ground bleeding and in terrible pain, and the next I was in Aric's father's kingdom. My wounds were gone and I could breathe again without difficulty. I felt younger and stronger than I have in years, Vani. The Kingdom of the Sky really is as beautiful as you said. As I stood up and began to look around I saw hundreds of others just like me. They were all confused, not sure where they were or what it meant. That little boy over there was with us too." She gestured to Ben, who was in the midst of telling his parents of his bizarre experience.

"And then we met him, Aric's father. He greeted us all and welcomed us to his kingdom. Then the ground beneath us began to shake. A Dove fluttered up, landed on the High King's shoulder and whispered in his ear. He nodded and dismissed the bird with a smile. Then he told us that we had died in the battle against Malik, but that he was going to send us back! At first I was sad, as I was getting used to the idea of calling the Kingdom of the Sky my new home. But then I thought of you, Vani. And of the others in Adhiren whom I love so much. And I knew that spending a little more time with you would be worth my while. There was a cold breeze, so powerful it swept all of us off our feet. Clouds flew past us, blocking our view of the kingdom. Then I opened my eyes and I was here."

"I'm so glad you came back." Vanessa wrapped Helena in a strong embrace.

Joyful reunions were taking place all over the

place that had so recently been a place of death and destruction. Loved ones who had run away with the Shadow Walkers rejoiced over seeing their friends again and being fully conscious of what they were doing for the first time in months. People who had been killed by the Shadow Walkers had also somehow returned and were alive and well. Naara was reunited with her parents and they were all happy and healthy. There was much crying and laughter as the people of Aric's Army were reunited with each other as they had been before Malik's horrid servants had appeared in their country. No one knew why it happened, but they were glad about it all the same.

Then an even bigger surprise occurred. Malik's non-human servants who had fallen also began to stand up. Vanessa gasped and drew her sword along with the other soldiers. She was surprised to see that her sword from Aric wasn't glowing, and the creatures did not seem to want to attack them. They looked just as confused as everyone else had been when they got up after the earthquake. They were examining themselves as if they had never seen their bodies before, with their horns, fur, claws, and other frightening features. Aric's soldiers laid down their weapons and some bravely went forward to attempt to communicate with the confused creatures.

A surprised gasp turned everyone's attention to the pit. "Look!" one of the soldiers cried. A man was crawling out, badly burned and beaten but alive. It was Aric.

Khalon and Tarak rushed over as fast as their legs

could take them to help their king.

"How did you survive?" Khalon asked as he grabbed onto one of Aric's arms.

"What happened?" Tarak asked as he took the other arm. Together they helped pull their king out of the pit. How he didn't die in the burning pit of lava was beyond them.

"Is Malik dead?" a young soldier asked.

Aric smiled at them and waited for the chatter to die down. The same light was emanating from him again, healing his wounds and making him look about ten years younger.

"Come and see," he said, beckoning to the edge of the pit.

All soldiers who were strong enough to walk gathered as close to the edge of the pit as they dared to stand and looked down to see a prison cell hovering over the burning lava. Blazing fire ran up and down the bars, and the solid iron lock had no hole for a key to be inserted. Inside, a sullen Malik was sulking, sitting with his knees pulled up to his chest.

"My father and I combined our powers to put Malik in his place," Aric explained. "He will not be able to escape this prison. His powers to communicate with his army through their thoughts has been significantly weakened." With a wave of his hand, Aric caused tonnes of obsidian and the ruins of Malik's palace to fall on the cage and all around it, until not a trace of it could be seen. The crowd backed away from the pit.

"The Shadow Walkers will not be bothering you

anymore. I have sent them away. One day, when my father is ready to welcome all of you into his kingdom and wipe the last remaining traces of evil from our land, he will open the cell and deal Malik his final punishment."

Sighs of relief came from every soldier gathered around the charred remains of Malik's stronghold.

"As for those of you who were led away by the Shadow Walkers," Aric said as he looked around at the bloodied and battered crowd, "I know that you did not understand what you were doing. You were lied to and mistreated. Malik took advantage of you. He has now been punished and is serving a life sentence for his crimes against you. If any of you wish to return to service in my army I would be more than happy to welcome you back. The same goes for those of you who used to serve under Malik if you wish to have a new king."

Typically this would have been a time for the crowd to raise their swords and cheer "Long live the king," but they were so exhausted as well as in awe of what Aric had done that for a long time there was nothing but silence on the battlefield. They looked at each other, and at Aric, with wide eyes and the occasional gasp or sigh. They didn't have the words to explain what they were experiencing. Aric sat a distance away from the crowd and smiled as he watched them.

Vanessa saw Jareth pull himself up and head in her direction.

"Will you be joining us again?" she asked Jareth with a smile.

"I don't know if I can." Jareth sighed. Tears were welling up in his eyes again.

"What do you mean?"

"I've done so many horrible things, Vanessa. I know you and your friends will be welcomed back into the army but I don't think I will be. How can someone who threatened, hurt and killed people Aric loves ever be accepted by him?"

"You heard what Aric said," Vanessa reassured her friend. "He understands that you did not know what you were doing. He has healed the people you hurt. He is not going to hold that against you. He knows you will not do that anymore. I'm sure he will welcome you back."

"I'm afraid he will be mad at me," Jareth said. "Will you come with me?"

"Of course." With one arm gently wrapped around Jareth, the two friends walked toward their king. Aric saw them coming and gave Jareth a warm smile. Jareth let go of Vanessa's arm and knelt in front of Aric.

"Sir," Jareth trembled as he bowed to the king. "I'm sorry I tried to hurt your people. I didn't know, I didn't understand...thank you for rescuing us. We really didn't deserve it. I've done and said so many horrible things."

King Aric reached out and put his hand on Jareth's face. The same light the High King had given him to fight Malik flowed from Aric's fingers into Jareth, and his face lit up like the sun. The cuts and bruises no longer looked fresh, but rather as if they had been healing for a couple of weeks. Jareth drew in a sharp breath, as if he were discovering breathing for the first time. Aric pulled his hand away and the light faded.

"Welcome back," Aric said, giving Jareth a firm handshake.

"Thank you Sir." A few tears ran down Jareth's face but for the first time in a long time, they were tears of joy and relief.

Vanessa turned around to see that more people were gathering around King Aric. Even many of Malik's creatures had come to pay respect to their rescuer. One by one they stepped forward, spoke to him, and were restored in the same manner that Jareth was. She even saw her father step forward. Before she knew what was happening, someone had grabbed her hand. She turned to see Arimay standing beside her with a smile on her face. "Come on!" she said.

Vanessa and Arimay got in line behind the others to speak to Aric. Arimay knelt in front of the king first. Aric smiled and reached out to touch her face. After the light had faded he turned and whispered something in his ear Vanessa couldn't hear. Then it was her turn.

"I'm sorry," Vanessa stammered, holding back her tears. "I'm sorry I wasn't able to fight harder, I'm sorry for when I've said hurtful things especially to my apprentice who you entrusted me with, I'm sorry I wasn't able to keep her safe…"

Aric stopped Vanessa and reached out to her. "You don't need to apologize for your weaknesses," Aric spoke gently. "Every soldier has them, in different ways. No one is perfect. There is no shame in making mistakes, for that is how you learn. I am proud of you."

Tears poured down Vanessa's face as she reached to embrace her king. "Thank you," she said, "thank you for everything." Then she let go and turned to move aside so other soldiers could approach their king. Apart from those speaking to King Aric, a reassuring silence had spread over most of the battlefield.

"Vanessa." Another familiar voice called to her. Vanessa turned around to see Dillan limping slowly toward her. He was covered in bruises, had a bloody lip and many cuts showing through his tattered clothes, but in that moment Vanessa couldn't think of having ever seen such a beautiful sight in her life.

"Dillan!" she cried, running to gently embrace him.

"We did it," Dillan said as he hugged her tighter. "We survived."

Tears of relief and joy poured from both of their faces.

"You mean Aric did it," Vanessa said, pulling away from Dillan slightly. "He's the reason we survived."

"And I'm so glad we did," Dillan said, moving to wipe a tear from Vanessa's face.

She was silent for a moment as she took in the sights all around her. Joyful reunions were happening everywhere she looked. There was laughter, embracing, and grateful tears as the injured, previously enslaved, and those who were thought to have been dead during the battle were reunited with their loved ones. *I never dreamed it would be possible* *for Malik's soldiers to want to serve Aric. But now we are seeing it with our own eyes. I wonder how many have been added to the army today? The only person I haven't seen yet is…*Brianna. *Where is she?*

A weak cough got Vanessa's attention. A weary-looking young lady with knotted, dirty blonde hair and a tattered dress came hobbling toward her. There were dark circles under her eyes and her face was covered in dirt, scratches, and bruises. *Do I know this person?*

"Vanessa," a raspy voice called. *Brianna!*

It was so unlike the way her friend usually presented herself. *The Shadow Walkers must have treated her very badly,* Vanessa realized with a shudder.

"I…" Brianna began. Her intense blue eyes stayed focused on the ground. "I am so sorry, Vanessa. I didn't mean what I said in the prison. You are not a bad friend. The Shadow Walkers were manipulating me and I couldn't see…"

"I understand," Vanessa replied, interrupting her friend's unnecessary apologies. She put her arm gently on Brianna's shoulder. "How is your mother? Did you find her?"

"She is alive." Brianna sighed, fresh tears rolling down her face. "The Shadow Walkers tortured her for many days. She almost died. But when Aric saved us she was freed. She is going to see him now."

"I am glad to hear that."

"I hope you can forgive me for what I did."

"Of course." Vanessa pulled her friend into an embrace. "It's been a difficult and confusing time for all of us. It's good to have you back. I'm glad you are safe now. Go and see Aric, he can take care of your wounds."

Brianna pulled away from her embrace with a slight nod and went to see their king.

"Arimay!" A familiar voice called out across the field. Vanessa and her apprentice turned to see the young Galemoorian man, Omari, stumbling toward them. One of his legs had been severely injured and he was limping. But from the light in his eyes and his big smile no one could tell he was in pain at all. Arimay ran toward him and Vanessa followed.

"It's you!" he gasped, reaching to hold the young apprentice's face in his hands. "Arimay, you're alive." He sat down as tears of relief began to run down his face.

"It's so good to see you." Arimay wept as she embraced him.

"There is still hope for our kingdom."

"For Adhiren? Of course there is. Aric is alive and all is well."

"No, Arimay," Omari clarified. "Not just for Adhiren. There is hope for Galemoor as well."

"What do you mean?" Arimay asked, puzzled. She pulled away from his embrace.

"You...you never knew your father," the kindly man said.

"No, but my mother said it was probably best that way."

"It was, at the time," Omari explained. "You see, I did not think we would live to see this day after all that

Malik had done. I figured there was no use telling you because everything seemed so hopeless..."

"Tell me what?"

Vanessa had sat down beside Arimay, intrigued by Omari's story.

"I know your father, Arimay. I spent a lot of time in the Galemoorian Palace, and I knew your mother well when she worked there as a servant. There was talk among the servants and a few rumours among the nobles but she confirmed it to me herself. Arimay, your father is Galemoor's king. Your father is King Ojas."

"What?" Arimay's mouth gaped open in shock.

"Your mother did not tell many people because the king ordered her not to. He said if people knew about their relationship it would bring disgrace to him and his family line. Your brother is part royal too. When your mother was pregnant with you she quit her job in the palace and looked for work elsewhere in the kingdom. She wanted to protect you and your brother."

"Why...why are you telling me this now, Omari?"

"Don't you see?" the man replied with great enthusiasm. "You have royal blood! The king has an heir of his own, but you have a legitimate claim to a position of authority in the government. Imagine, one day, a ruler of Galemoor who can tell our people about King Aric and change the laws that have made so many suffer for so many years."

Arimay's eyes grew wide as she stood in stunned silence. After a few moments she cleared her throat and did her best to respond to the sudden revelation: "I don't think I can be the ruler you've hoped for, Omari. At least not right now. We just fought Malik and the Shadow Walkers and we didn't think we would survive that. And I'm only ten! This is...this is a lot to think about. I don't think I'm ready to fight for a position in the government of Galemoor. I am not strong enough or brave enough for that yet."

"All in due time, Dear One," Omari smiled at Arimay. "Whatever you decide, I and your fellow Galemoorian members of Aric's Army will be here to support you."

"Thank you, Omari."

"Now I must go to see Aric." He winced as the pain in his injured leg grew stronger. "Will you help me?"

"Of course." Arimay and her mentor helped Omari stand up and led him to the king.

Those who had been healed set to work tending to the others who were severely wounded and could not get to Aric on their own. After a few hours nearly everyone had made their way to Aric and re-dedicated themselves to serving in his army. The only one who didn't was Bogdan, who decided to remain in the ruins of Hadriar and live a life of solitude in honour of his master.

"I am glad to have you all back together at last," Aric spoke as the crowd of restored soldiers gathered around him. "It has been far too long, and I'm sorry for the suffering you experienced in the meantime. Life is going to be much better from now on. With Malik permanently imprisoned, there will be peace in our land. You will be free to do more of the things you used to enjoy before the Shadow Walkers came. Of course, I still expect everyone to keep up with their training." He smiled as laughter came from many of the people gathered. "But before we get back to those things, I think we should have a celebration!"

The crowd cheered and raised their swords.

"One week from now I will hold the biggest banquet Emeraldia has ever seen, to celebrate victory over Malik and the return and addition of so many of you to my army. It will be held at my palace beginning at sundown. Everyone will be welcome to attend. As soon as we return to Adhiren we will begin making preparations."

The crowd dispersed and began to gather up the few belongings they had left. The few whose horses hadn't run away or been killed went to tend to their animals and prepare them to leave. Soon a long line of soldiers had started their procession back toward their home. The clouds had parted and the sun was shining almost as bright as the light that had restored Aric and the others to their former strength.

Vanessa looked up at the Doves flying above them on their journey home. *Aric really did have a plan after all,* she realized. *He defeated Malik and saved us. I never should have doubted him.*

Vanessa and Arimay walked together as the crowd headed for Gal'Mesh.

"A royal." Arimay sighed. "Imagine that!"

"You have a strength inside you unlike any other," Vanessa said. "And I'm sure Aric and Omari have seen that in you all along. Whatever you decide, I know you will do great things."

"What will we do when we get back to our homes?"

"Rest for a day or two, I reckon."

"And then what? There are no more battles to fight. What will all the soldiers do now?"

"I don't know," Vanessa said, meeting her gaze.

The group stopped for water and a rest outside the gates of Gal'Mesh. When people heard they had visitors from Aric's Army they ran out to meet them and stopped in their tracks with gaping mouths. They weren't severely injured. They weren't dead. There were more of them than there had been heading into Tar'Máran. *How could that be?*

They surrounded the soldiers of Aric and bombarded them with questions. One by one they told the Gal'Meshans about what they had seen and what Aric had done. Some said it was nonsense and turned back into the city murmuring about hallucinations. But many stayed and asked to speak with Aric. One by one, Vanessa saw them kneel as Aric tapped his sword lightly on both of their shoulders, stamped his crest on their right hands and asked them to rise.

They're joining us!

Even Lennea, the Guardian of Gal'Mesh, had come to see the king. When the chatter died down she addressed the crowd: "People of Adhiren, what we have seen before us today is truly unlike anything we have ever seen or heard. I, as well as the rest of you, know now and believe that Aric and his father the High King are truly powerful and that they truly care for those who serve them. That is why, as Guardian of this city, today I declare that we will raise the Crest of Aric at the city gates, in honour of the great terror he and his people have saved us from today."

Cheers rose up from the crowd. There were tears of joy as Aric's Army celebrated this news and welcomed even more people into their ranks. Aric told them about the upcoming celebration and they decided to pack what they could carry and join the rest of the army on the way to Emeraldia immediately.

CHAPTER FOURTEEN

IT WAS PAST MIDNIGHT WHEN Aric and his army approached the gates of Emeraldia. Excited chatter rippled through the crowd as they beheld the gates of the city many of them feared they would never see again. A large crowd had gathered at the gates and were waiting for them with flowers and confetti. They cheered as they saw the army approach the gates.

"Aric has won!" they cheered. "Aric has defeated Malik! Welcome home, Army of Aric!"

The joyful procession made their way through the city with only a small amount of lit torches to lead the way. Music of flutes, fiddles and trumpets proclaimed the arrival of the victorious group. Although most of the buildings looked like dark lumps in the shadows, the atmosphere in Emeraldia made it seem as if it were the middle of the day. The soldiers' exhaustion temporarily disappeared as they celebrated their victory and their return home. They marched and danced through the city and up the plateau to King

Aric's majestic palace.

"Oh no." Arimay gasped. Vanessa and the rest of the soldiers stopped in their tracks, mouths gaping open. What lay before them was so devastating that for a moment they were all at a loss for words.

"The palace!" Faylon cried. "It's ruined!"

What Faylon had said was true: through the flickers of torchlight the Army of Aric could see bricks and other various pieces of the once-great palace scattered across the plateau. The only part that remained intact was the arched entrance. It looked as if the palace had been split in two and collapsed on itself. Many other buildings in the city had suffered damage, but not as much as Aric's home had.

"The earthquake must have reached here," Aric replied. He walked over to the arch and placed his hand on it gently, as if too much pressure would cause it to collapse as well. "This palace served us well for many years, and the celebrations held here will long be remembered."

"What are you going to do now?" Ben asked. "Where are you going to live, King Aric?"

"Do not worry about me," Aric reassured the child with a smile. "I do not require a palace to live in. I am happy to live among you wherever that may be. I will ask the strongest of my soldiers to assist me in removing what materials we can salvage from the palace in the coming days. I am sure there are many things we can re-use that will be useful for our celebration."

"We are still going to have the celebration?" one

woman asked. "How?"

"My palace may have been destroyed, but all of you are alive and that is what's most important to me," Aric said. "We will have the banquet somewhere else. We shall set up everything we need in the Emera Fields one week from today. Bring your tents and any food you have to share. This will still be the greatest celebration this country has ever seen!"

Cheers rose up from the crowd. They raised their swords and torches and called out "Long live the king!"

"Now you must all get some rest," Aric said gently. "We have all worked very hard these last few days and will need our strength to prepare for our celebration. Those of you in Emeraldia with homes that were not destroyed, please make room for a few additional guests tonight. Those in Kalmehara may need to host additional guests as well for the time being, as our numbers have increased greatly today."

"We will do as you say," Tarak spoke for the crowd, bowing to his king. "Thank you for everything you have done for us, King Aric."

The crowd dispersed as everyone went to their homes to rest and begin preparations for the big celebration.

* * *

A week later, Vanessa and her friends walked through the bustling city full of Aric's soldiers preparing for the grand banquet. Some soldiers, with the help of the

Tigrés, carried tables out to the field and set them up in long rows for the food to be prepared and served on. The Gal'Meshans brought their finest tents to cover the area and provide shelter for those who would be staying the night. A large wooden platform was built in front of an area of the field that had been cleared and set aside specifically for dancing. Musicians got together and practiced their songs. The Doves carried branches and sweet-smelling flowers in their beaks and draped them over the tables and tents. Aric supervised it all with a smile on his face.

"I can't wait for the banquet," Arimay said, twirling around in her favourite red and gold dress.

"It will come soon enough," Vanessa said. "Which dress should I wear?"

"Definitely the pink and white one," Arimay said. Her eyes had a dreamy look about them, as if she were lost in another place. "It will look beautiful on you."

"Thanks." Vanessa smiled and sat down on a bench. Arimay sat beside her.

"How are you going to do your hair for the banquet?" she asked.

"I don't know," Vanessa replied with a shrug. "However I feel like doing it that day I guess."

"But Vanessa," Arimay's eyes widened as her voice took on a serious tone. "This banquet is a *big deal*."

Vanessa laughed. "Remember how I told you that each one of Aric's banquets is better than the one that came before it? You'll get used to it soon enough."

"I don't think I'll ever get used to how amazing they are."

"The point is, Arimay," Vanessa continued, "it's about having fun. I feel beautiful at the banquets even if I don't have the most fancy hair. I want to live in the moment and enjoy the celebration, and not worry about how I look."

"But don't you want to impress Dillan?"

Vanessa blushed. "I'm pretty sure Dillan will still be my friend regardless of what my hair looks like."

"Fine, that's your choice then," Arimay said. She resumed twirling around in her dress and admiring how the gold embroidery shone in the afternoon sun. "I'm going to dance all night!"

"I'm sure you are," Vanessa replied. "But we've got a few more chores to finish before we can think about dancing all night. Come on." The two soldiers headed back to Kalmehara, where they had promised they would help Alexander clean and get the horses ready for the big night.

* * *

The Emera Fields buzzed with excitement as Aric's great celebration got underway. Floating lanterns were released into the night sky by hundreds of giggling children, casting a warm glow over the celebrations. The sweet smell of flowers mixed with the aromas of roasting meat and freshly baked bread. Across the field the music of various musicians combined to form one glorious and beautiful song in honour of the king. The Doves and Tigrés were circling overhead, swooping and twirling as they joined in the celebrations the best ways that they knew how.

Tables as far as the eye could see had been set up in rows where bakers and chefs were working hard putting the finishing touches on delicious platters for their guests. Tender meats were roasting over open fires. Bowls of steaming hot vegetables glazed in a sweet sauce were being served alongside rolls of freshly baked Pinnamari Bread. Fresh mangoes, apples, pears and Rubiberries were displayed surrounding chocolate puddings. There were even cakes in every hue of the rainbow, covered in rich chocolate or vanilla frosting. As Vanessa and her friends were admiring the food, an older boy spinning a roasted pig over a spit caught her eye. *I've seen him before,* she realized.

"Hey Vanessa!" the boy greeted with a large smile on his face.

"Hello," Vanessa replied. "I know we have met before, but I can't seem to remember your name."

"I'm Ethan," the boy replied as he turned to make sure the meat was cooking to perfection. "I was at the first banquet you ever came to in Adhiren, remember? I was cleaning up the dishes from your table and I…"

"You tripped and fell over on a banana peel!" Vanessa finished. The two laughed as they recalled the memory. "That was quite the mess wasn't it?"

"Not one of my finest moments," Ethan replied with a smile.

"It's nice to see you again," Vanessa replied.

"Same to you," Ethan replied. "I am still working in

the king's kitchen. Or, I guess, I *used* to work in the king's kitchen...cooking is my thing now. I never was very coordinated with the dishes."

"Well it looks like you are doing a wonderful job," Vanessa said with a smile. "I can't wait to try everything!"

"I reckon you won't have to wait long," Ethan replied. "Word is Aric is going to get things started very soon."

"Vanessa!" Arimay shrieked with excitement. "Come here! There's a cake shaped like an emerald and it's bigger than Gaerwin's head!" The young apprentice grabbed her mentor's hand and dragged her away from where Ethan was standing.

Vanessa waved and gave Ethan an apologetic smile as she was whisked away to examine the dessert that had captured Arimay's attention. Ethan nodded politely and returned to his work.

"It's so big," Arimay said in awe as she gazed at the shiny green creation. "I have never seen a cake this big before."

"I bet Gaerwin could eat it all," Vanessa joked, gently nudging her friend.

"I definitely could," Gaerwin added, "if I wasn't also saving room for the chicken and potatoes!"

The group stood transfixed by the array of carefully crafted treats as cooks rushed around them. It wasn't long before a trumpet blast signaled the beginning of the evening's festivities and Vanessa and her friends went to find their seats. Dillan rushed in quickly, nudging his way through the group to get a seat next to Vanessa.

"Where were you?" Vanessa asked. "It's unusual for you to be late for a banquet."

"I'm not late," Dillan protested, wiping the sweat off his brow. "Just ran into a few soldiers I haven't trained with in awhile, that's all. They were a very talkative bunch. We were way over by the musicians there." He pointed. "So I had to run."

Vanessa gently placed one of her hands over Dillan's on the table as he regained his normal breathing. "Well, after all that running you must be hungry."

"I sure am!" Dillan replied with a smile.

The crowd fell silent as Aric stepped up on the wooden platform, with Khalon and Tarak at his sides as well as two Tigrés. The Emera Fields had never looked so grand. "Welcome," Aric began, "to the largest gathering of the Army of Aric that Adhiren has ever seen! It is my privilege to welcome here today both long-serving members of my army as well as the thousands of new recruits who have joined us this past week."

Cheers erupted from the Gal'Meshans and former soldiers of Malik who cheerfully raised their glasses and called out, "Long live the king!"

"In the coming weeks we will discuss how to repair the damage done to the great city of Emeraldia and how we will proceed with training from now on. But for today, let us celebrate the victory over Malik and that we can all gather together in peace without fear of the Shadow Walkers."

More cheers.

"Those who have prepared the banquet for us today

have done an incredible job with the limited resources they were given. Let us thank them and enjoy our Celebration of Peace!"

The crowd clapped and cheered as they rose from their seats and walked toward the delicious smells that had captured their attention from the moment they had arrived at the banquet. Vanessa and her friends filled their plates and spent the evening talking and laughing over many glasses of Rubiberry juice.

When the meal was over, the music began. Groups of soldiers as well as individuals took the stage for many hours to play and sing songs dedicated to King Aric and his victory in Tar'Máran. One song blended seamlessly into the next, as if each individual performer had been given a small piece of a much larger song and had planned the unity between the pieces in advance. While Vanessa and her friends were dancing they heard the familiar deep voice of Faylon singing with the flutes and fiddles:

In the shadows of the night
When terror comes to steal the light
We will raise our swords with a mighty yell
Courage, courage, all is well!
Courage, courage, all is well!
Malik wants to feed your fear
But Aric and Doves are always near
His power we to the creatures tell
Courage, courage, all is well!
Courage, courage, all is well!

He then continued with a third verse he had written for the celebration:

Malik in The Pit is he
Lies he can no longer tell
Aric has the victory
Peace, Adhiren, all is well!
Peace, Adhiren, all is well!

Vanessa stopped for a moment after the song had finished to catch her breath. She had been spinning around with Brianna and Arimay and had completely lost sight of Dillan. *Where is he? I'm sure he was here a moment ago.*

A moment later, Dillan snuck up behind her. "You scared me!" Vanessa cried out, punching him in the arm.

"May I have this dance?" he asked, bowing gracefully with a silly expression on his face.

Vanessa's blushed and smiled. "Of course, young man."

As Vanessa and Dillan danced, she turned to see if Aric would be joining them. She noticed the cheerful expression had disappeared from his face. Her king looked sad. *What is there to be sad about on a night like this?*

CHAPTER FIFTEEN

"*I STILL CAN'T BELIEVE* this is happening," Vanessa said to Dillan as they danced gracefully to the music playing in the fields.

"Well believe it." Dillan smiled, "life will be better from now on. No more nightmares, no more wars, no more torture. Just more of this," he gestured to the rest of Aric's Army that surrounded them everywhere they could see.

"I think I will like this new life very much."

Their quiet moment together was soon interrupted by a frantic tugging on Vanessa's dress. She turned around to see Arimay waving and trying to get her attention.

"Sorry to interrupt this moment but there's something you need to see," she said matter-of-factly. She took hold of Vanessa's arm and pointed in the direction of the stage. Vanessa turned to see what had caught the attention of her apprentice. Through the dancing crowd she could see King Aric, Khalon, Tarak, and two Tigrés. The typically joyful and sociable king had a serious expression on his face. He and the small group gathered with him turned their backs to the large gathering and began to walk further into the field, away from the noise.

"What are they doing?"

"I have no idea. This isn't like Aric. He is usually right here in the middle of the celebration. He looked sad for a moment earlier too and I don't know why."

"Want to go find out?"

"I don't know, Arimay. They might want to have a private conversation. Maybe it isn't any of our business."

Before Vanessa had finished speaking, Arimay had grabbed her by the hand and started leading her toward the secretive group.

"Whether it's my business or not," she said, "something serious is going on here. Someone needs to investigate! Plus, I've never been this close to a Tigré before. They are so beautiful!"

"Vanessa! Where are you going?" Dillan called, noticing his dancing partner was leaving him. He met Vanessa's puzzled gaze through the crowd and ran to catch up with her and Arimay. Soon Jareth and Gaerwin were following as well. They ran past the stage and into an area of the field that had not been used for the celebrations. In the flurry of activity on the dance floor their strange behaviour was hardly noticed. The dancing and singing continued on as if no one had seen Aric leave.

They slowed their pace as they neared Aric, his army commanders and the Tigrés. Aric's group was standing in a circle, all eyes on him as he spoke in a low, soft tone. The warm night air and starry sky created a calming silence around them, broken only by what Vanessa and her friends could hear of the king's conversation. The music of the banquet sounded faded as if it were miles away from the patch of long grass in which they were silently huddled. Vanessa had many different feelings rush through her as she sat there, but she couldn't put words to what it all meant. Something very important was about to happen, but no one knew what it was. Sensing her tension, Arimay reached out to hold Vanessa's hand as they sat and tried to catch pieces of the discussion.

"It makes sense, Your Majesty, but why now?"

"Now is the time my father has chosen, Tarak. Malik is under control and you should have peace in Adhiren for a very long time. I will not be needed here as often as I have been in the past."

"But we *will* still need you."

"That is why the Doves are staying here. They will, as they have always, serve as messengers between myself and all the members of my army. You can contact me anytime you need to, and I will send instructions to you when I need to."

"It won't be the same without you physically here, my king. That will take a long time for the rest of your army to get used to."

"Where is Aric going?" Arimay whispered.

"Shhhhh!" Vanessa turned to Arimay and signaled to her to be quiet. A Tigré looked up, ears twitching as it detected Arimay's whisper. After a quick glance around the area it settled back down, content that no danger was present.

"Yes, it will be difficult for them at first," Aric agreed. "But they are strong, supportive people and I have no doubt they will continue to look after each other even in the midst of this time of adjustment."

"How long will you be away?" Khalon asked the king.

"My father has not yet made that clear," Aric replied. "But our work will take awhile to complete. I may not return until after you yourself have arrived in the Kingdom of the Sky."

Arimay gasped. Vanessa's eyes widened. *What was so important that Aric would have to be away for so long?*

As Vanessa and her friends pondered what this strange conversation might mean, they saw an ornamented staircase begin to descend from the sky. It sparkled and shone in the starlight as if it were made of diamonds. Slowly, very slowly, two feet began to descend the stairs. Soon legs came into view, then a chest, then a face Vanessa recognized at once. It was Aric's father, the High King of the World!

He was dressed in dazzling white robes with a purple sash. He wore a silver crown on his head that was covered in emeralds and sapphires. His deep blue eyes seemed to be smiling as he looked at his son and the small group gathered with him. He stepped off the staircase and stood beside his son, putting an arm around Aric's shoulder. He was much taller than Aric, but their resemblance was uncanny.

"Well, son," the High King's magnificent voice boomed, "are you ready?"

"Yes, father," Aric replied, with his face shining in the light of the dazzling staircase, "I'm ready."

"Ready for what?" Arimay whispered.

Vanessa stared at her apprentice open-mouthed and shrugged. *I have no clue what he's doing.*

"Then I must bid you farewell for now," Aric said. "You have served me well, and I have no doubt that you will serve the people of Adhiren well in the days, weeks, and years to come. Though it may seem like a long time that we will be apart, know that the work my father and I are doing is so that we do not have to be away from you forever."

Khalon and Tarak both stepped forward to embrace Aric. The Tigrés approached their king and bowed, allowing him to gently stroke the top of their heads.

"We will miss you, King Aric," Tarak spoke with his head bowed.

"We will do everything you have instructed," Khalon promised.

"I know you will. You are both fine leaders. Do not be discouraged, my friends. When this world is about to face its end, you will see me again."

Aric turned to mount the stairway with his father, which led back into the Kingdom of the Sky. They waved to the small group below. As they climbed higher and higher, a bright light encompassed them and within moments they were gone. The Tigrés and the commanders bowed silently in respect, and remained in silence for a couple of moments. Then, at Khalon's signal, the group turned and headed back in the direction of the festivities.

Vanessa and her friends sat in stunned silence as they tried to process what they had seen and heard.

Arimay was no longer asking questions. Tears were rolling down her face.

"He didn't even say goodbye to us," she sighed. Vanessa pulled Arimay into an embrace. A tear rolled down her face as well.

For what seemed like hours the group of friends stared into the night sky, eyes wide. They were so focused on trying to figure out what happened that they didn't notice the other group approach until Khalon said "Hey, what are you folks doing here?"

"Huh?" Vanessa's attention snapped back to the present moment. She looked up to see Khalon standing over her with an amused expression on his face.

"Oh, Khalon, Sir," Arimay stuttered as she stood up and brushed off her dress. Her friends quickly stood as well in a show of respect to the Tigrés and the army commanders. "We saw you and Aric and the Tigrés walking away from the party and it seemed a little odd, so we....well, we followed you to see what was going on."

As Vanessa stood up and met Khalon's gaze she could see the commander had a tear running down his cheek.

"Your curiosity has been noted on many occasions, young one," Khalon replied. "You must learn to be careful though. It may get you into trouble someday."

"Yes, Sir." Arimay turned her gaze to the ground.

"I don't blame you for being curious," Tarak added with a smile. "What just happened was a rather unusual event indeed. Nothing like it has ever happened in Adhiren before. What all did you hear?"

"That Aric is going away," Dillan said.

"Something about important work," Gaerwin added.

"He may not come back for a long time," Vanessa said as her voice began to tremble.

"He didn't say goodbye," Arimay added.

"He's going with his father to the Kingdom of the Sky," Dillan finished.

"But why?" Jareth asked.

The group sat down together and Khalon and Tarak began to fill in the missing pieces.

"As you have probably noticed, Aric's Army has grown exponentially in the past week." Khalon nodded in the direction of the banquet. "And that is a wonderful thing. There is no limit to how many people may join; all are welcome here in Adhiren."

"I still can't believe Malik's former soldiers and the people of Gal'Mesh all wanted to join so quickly," Arimay said.

"Yes." Khalon chuckled. "It is quite a marvelous thing."

"Maybe the entire city of Galemoor will join Aric someday too!"

"I would like that very much," Khalon replied.

"So would I."

"But because of this growth," Tarak added, "Aric and his father have some more work to do. Do you remember when they combined their power to defeat Malik?"

The soldiers nodded in unison. How could they forget such a marvelous sight?

"Well, when Aric and his father work together, they can do much more than that. The light they create when they combine their power gives them the ability to create anything they want. And so now, the time has come that they must return to the Kingdom of the Sky and expand it, so that there will be room for everyone who serves in his newly expanded army."

"Expand?" Arimay asked.

"Yes. Aric told us that he and his father are going to add more buildings, more meadows, forests and valleys, all beautiful things for us to enjoy, all more beautiful than anything that has ever been made in Adhiren. That way, he and his father will never have to turn anyone away who chooses to serve in his army."

"It sounds like a wonderful place." Arimay sighed. "I can't wait to see it someday."

"It really is quite amazing," Vanessa added, recalling her brief visit there during the Battle of the Emera Fields.

"So, now that Aric is with his father," Dillan interjected, "who will be in charge of his army while he's away?"

"Good question," Tarak replied. "Our king has made preparations for every area of army life in his absence. He has split the main leadership roles between Khalon and myself." he gestured to his fellow commander, "and we will be in charge of assigning new commanders and overseeing training. We will both preside over soldier naming ceremonies as well."

"So, is Aric going to communicate with you directly

then?" Jareth asked.

"Dear young man," Khalon laughed, "he will still be able to communicate with all of you! The Doves are still here, and they are still his messengers as they have always been. We will not have exclusive rights to communicate with Aric. And the way I see it, that's for the best. We need each and every one of you to support us in our new roles, and to challenge us if you ever think we are being selfish or unfair. Otherwise, with such power it can be tempting to rule Adhiren our way instead of Aric's, and if you recall what happened to Malik I'm sure you can imagine that would only lead to trouble. Do you understand?"

"Yes," Vanessa replied as she and her peers nodded. "We will support you, Khalon and Tarak. I'm sure you will be great leaders."

"You have been a great leader too," Tarak replied. "You, Arimay, Dillan, Gaerwin and Jareth. I am proud to say that Aric's Army contains such fine young people. We will need your strength in the days to come."

"Why didn't Aric tell everyone about this at the banquet?" Jareth asked.

"His people have suffered so much as of late." Khalon replied, "he decided it was best to allow them to continue celebrating for the rest of the night. Besides, if he had tried to explain this in that large of a crowd, he would have been overwhelmed with questions and never get to finishing what he had to say. People would have tried to stop him from leaving, and it would have turned into a chaotic mess."

"So are you...are you going to go tell them now?"

"Yes." Khalon sighed as he stood. "That duty has fallen to Tarak and I."

"That won't be an easy task," Arimay sympathized.

"No," Khalon replied, "but it is my honour to serve my King in this way, as you have all served him in your own ways."

"People are definitely going to freak out," Jareth stated.

"I'll help stop the riots if there are any!" Gaerwin offered.

"Your support is greatly appreciated," Tarak said, looking around at the faithful group of young soldiers. "All of you. Whatever you can do to calm the fears of your fellow army members at this time would be greatly appreciated."

The loyal soldiers of Aric stood and turned to head back to the banquet. The Tigrés surrounded them as they walked toward the wooden platform to make one of the most bizarre announcements Adhiren would ever hear.

Vanessa gave Khalon and Tarak each a firm handshake, and Dillan and the others followed suit. As they turned to rejoin the crowd, Vanessa met Khalon's gaze. "Long live the king," she said.

"Yes." Khalon smiled as he ascended the stage. "Long live the king."

* * *

Vanessa and her friends decided to hang back from

the emotional crowd for a bit as they tried to process everything they had seen and heard in the past week. They would all miss Aric, but seeing what happened firsthand gave them a sense of peace about the situation that the other soldiers did not currently have.

"So what's next for you?" Jareth asked Vanessa. "Now that there are no battles to fight?"

"I think I'll be perfectly content to take it easy for awhile," Vanessa replied. "What about you?"

"I'm going to do what I can to help clean out more of the wreckage in Emeraldia," Jareth replied. "Maybe Aurelio will let me work for him again."

"I'm sure he will."

"What about you, Arimay?" Brianna asked. "Are you going to claim your position in the Galemoorian court?"

Arimay laughed. "Maybe someday. I don't think I'm ready for that yet."

"We're happy to have you with us for as long as you want to stay."

"Gaerwin," Arimay asked, "what are you doing to do?"

"I'm not sure," the young man replied. "I would like to get married someday, settle down and have my own home in Emeraldia. But right now I could really go for some more of that delicious cake!"

Vanessa laughed. "Go for it." Gaerwin stepped away from the group for a moment to enjoy the remnants of the great feast.

"I'm going to miss Aric." Arimay sighed.

"Me too," Vanessa agreed, putting her hand on Arimay's shoulder. "We all will."

"At least you got to spend a couple of years with him," Arimay replied. "It feels like I just arrived here. There's still so much I don't know. And I hardly got to talk with him after my naming ceremony."

"We can still talk to Aric," Alexander replied, joining the conversation. "That is why the Doves are still here with us, remember?" He motioned to the tent he was carrying and pointed to a place in the distance where he was headed to set it up.

"I'll come help you in a minute," Vanessa promised. She and Arimay bid their friends goodnight and followed Alexander.

"Did you know Aric was going to leave?" Arimay asked as she helped spread out the colourful Kalmeharan fabric.

"No, young one, I did not know."

"Then why are you so calm? Everyone else is so upset."

"I have learned from a lifetime of experience that Aric's plans are always for the best, even when they don't make sense to us. If his leaving means a better life for us in the end, then I am content to adjust to the changes. And we know the Doves and army commanders will remain here and I trust they will lead us well."

"I know." Arimay sighed, resting her head on her hand. "It's just not the same."

"How do you think the others are handling the news?" Vanessa asked her father.

"Well as you saw out there earlier, there may be quite a bit of chaos for a few days," Alexander replied. "Most of the soldiers did not have the benefit of speaking with Khalon and Tarak before the announcement was made. It's going to take all of us some time to adjust to the new way that our lives will work here in Adhiren."

"I hope everything will turn out alright," Arimay said.

"I'm sure it will," Vanessa reassured her apprentice. "It will take some time. And we will help by telling people what we have seen and heard." She turned to leave the tent. "I'm going to help some of our friends set up their tents. I'll be back soon!"

"Long live the king," Arimay whispered as she pulled a blanket up to her shoulders.

"Long live the king," Vanessa replied with a smile.

Moments after Vanessa had left, a fluttering sound startled Arimay. She sat up to see a Dove standing on her legs, cooing contentedly.

"Hi," Arimay whispered. "Do you have a message for me?"

"Greetings, servant of Aric," the Dove spoke. "I came to see you because I sensed you had a message you wished to send to the king."

"Yes." Arimay nodded. She gently placed her hand on the birds head and whispered in its ear: "Please take care of my family. Tell them I will come back for them someday. And please tell Aric to come back soon."

Aric to the Sky Kingdom has gone
Adhiren he will still look upon

You have his deeds and stories to tell
Peace, Adhiren, all is well!
Peace, Adhiren, all is well!

Acknowledgments

A Whisper in the Shadows has been fifteen years in the making. I first created the character of Arimay in 2009, around the time I started the second draft of *The Necklace*. I didn't find the place where she fit into the story until years later.

This story was influenced by events in my own life, as well as many sermons and Bible study discussions I heard during this time about not being complacent with the evil that exists in this world, and staying together to pray and encourage each other to stay strong. The good news is that in the end, evil doesn't win!

Once again, my faithful peer editors gave me lots of valuable feedback on multiple drafts of this book. Thank you Chrissy and Jennine for all your help! From catching important missing words to finding leftover scenes from previous versions, A Whisper in the Shadows would not be in its best form without your help.

I must also thank Ruth Buchanan of Build a Better Us for her professional edits and feedback on an earlier version of this story.

Thank you to the students at Westmount School in Moose Jaw, Saskatchewan who always asked me when the sequel to *The Necklace* was going to be finished, and asked me to sign their math worksheets because they thought I was famous. Your encouragement meant a lot to me!

Dariia, my cover designer, did it again, making an amazing cover featuring one of my favourite scenes in the book that I hope you love as much as I do. Thank you for your hard work that made this story come to life!

My friend Lisa, for lending me her art supplies to make my beautiful map.

To the real "Lady Katharine": I can't believe it's been 18 years since you left us. I've always wanted to give your name to a minor character in a book. I imagine you as she is—beautiful, happy, and healthy, dancing in the real Kingdom of the Sky. I am looking forward to seeing you again someday.

And Brittany. I had hoped you would be around to read this book. I'm sure you would have liked it. Though you left too soon I take comfort in knowing that you are now among the "Great Cloud of Witnesses" (Hebrews 12:1) in the real Kingdom of the Sky.

And last (but not least), thank you Jesus for giving me the inspiration to write and share this story. My life would not be the same without you! Thank you for your ultimate sacrifice that gives us freedom and reminds us that evil will one day be defeated.

About The Author

Amy Smart grew up in Port Elgin, Ontario. Some of her favourite books growing up included The Chronicles of Narnia by C. S. Lewis and The Warriors series by Erin Hunter. She also enjoyed writing from a young age, and began writing her own short stories when she was six years old. In her adult years (so far) Amy has moved to southern Saskatchewan, attended Briercrest College and Seminary, and currently works taking care of animals. She lives with her two cats Louie and Stormy. She is continuing to work on her books and looking forward to her next writing adventure!

Thanks for reading! Please add a short review on Amazon or Goodreads and let me know what you thought!

Subscribe to my monthly newsletter! Send me an email at amysmartbooks@gmail.com to subscribe. You can also send me any questions or comments you have about my books. I would love to hear from you!